END GAME

A gripping crime thriller full of breathtaking twists

CHARLIE GALLAGHER

JOFFE BOOKS

Published 2017 by Joffe Books, London.

www.joffebooks.com

© Charlie Gallagher

This book is a work of fiction. Names, characters, businesses, organizations, places and events are either the product of the author's imagination or are used fictitiously. Any resemblance to actual persons, living or dead, events or locales is entirely coincidental. The spelling is British English.

All rights reserved. No part of this publication may be reproduced, stored in retrieval system, copied in any form or by any means, electronic, mechanical, photocopying, recording or otherwise transmitted without written permission from the publisher. You must not circulate this book in any format.

ISBN-13: 978-1-912106-89-9

For Johnny C. Who wouldn't let me quit.

Author's Note

I am inspired by what I do and see in my day job as a front-line police detective, though my books are entirely fictional. I am aware that the police officers in my novels are not always shown positively. They are human and they make mistakes. This is sometimes the case in real life too, but the vast majority of officers are honest and do a good job in trying circumstances. From what I see on a daily basis, the men and women who wear the uniform are among the very finest, and I am proud to be part of one of the best police forces in the world.

Charlie Gallagher

Chapter 1

His wife straightened herself and backed away, beaming at him through the screen. He could only see parts of the kitchen in the background — the island work surface with its oversized tap arcing from the centre, and the large window beyond. She leaned against the island and looked directly at him. The kitchen was newly finished, the heart of the home and her pride and joy.

'Is that better?'

'Much better. I can see you now!'

For a second and then she was just a silhouette. Sunlight poured through the window behind her and filled the room.

'Shut up! I'm a mess. I've not even put my face on.'

He made a show of checking his watch and opening his mouth in mock horror.

'It's nearly nine, Shelley!'

'It's half eight.'

'Close enough.'

'At least I've done my hair.' Shelley raised a hand to the tightly wrapped headscarf. Her hair loss had been sudden, almost immediately after the first treatment.

'I like it. It's a new one, right?'

Shelley nodded. 'Yup. Matches nicely with the top.' Shelley wore a white T-shirt with a large *YSL* emblem on the front. She'd spotted it on her way out of the treatment centre and he'd bought it for her as a treat.

Some days were better than others. Today she was smiling, almost upbeat. Whenever he could get into the privacy of his office, he used the video streaming feature on his phone so he could see and talk to her. He told her he just liked to see his beautiful wife, but they both knew he was checking up on her, making sure that she really was okay. Because when she wasn't, there was no hiding it.

She had slept for a few hours. It was amazing what a difference it made. He had needed to tiptoe out of the room this morning. Normally, when his alarm woke him, she would already be downstairs, waiting for him with a weak smile and a strong coffee.

The aura surrounding his wife darkened. A figure passed close to the window and he rolled his eyes in irritation.

'And you can tell your mum to leave our garden alone! I told her I'll get out there myself, but it will have to wait till spring.'

Now he could make out her scowl.

'I told her.'

'I can see she's out there. You should tell her to stay away from the window.'

His wife twisted round to look out. 'Don't worry. She's not coming till one.'

'I saw her in the garden!'

He shook his head, smiling. He had caught them out. Her mother would be fussing over Shelley and pottering in the garden all day. It would finish up cluttered with hanging signs and cutesy ornaments, just like hers.

His wife went over to the window. 'Oh yeah, there is someone.'

He had to strain now to hear her through the tiny speakers. She turned towards the back door. A lot of their friends used this entrance rather than come to the front. The door was out of sight but he could see his wife. She stopped and reached out to open it. Then she stepped back.

'Can I help you?' He could hear she sounded nervous even through the tiny speakers. The man watching from twenty miles away tensed and called out.

'Shelley! Honey, lock the door and talk to them through the window. Shelley?'

She didn't turn, didn't acknowledge him. She had frozen. Was it the camera? Then she moved — there was nothing wrong with the picture. Shelley was backing away from whoever was at the door. She held her arms out as if to placate them. She looked scared.

'What . . . what do you want?'

He jumped to his feet and stood watching his phone. It lay on its side. On the screen, his wife walked backwards across their kitchen. He fought the urge to shout out. It would achieve nothing and he didn't want to risk being cut off.

A hand in a black leather glove came into view on the far left side of his screen. It held a small axe. Hand and axe moved forward. His wife had come to a halt, backed up against their new cooker, only just in his view. The figure now appeared at the opposite end of the screen, moving forward slowly and deliberately. The man was dressed in black, with a balaclava that revealed a slither of white skin in the eye holes. The man walked in front of the window, and the screen went dark, like an eclipse, then the camera slowly refocussed.

His wife's hands dropped to her side. He saw her eyes dart around the kitchen. There was a knife block to her right, dead centre of his screen. The intruder was probably closer but if she was fast she could get to it first. But that axe. No, she didn't stand a chance.

The axe was held high. It glinted in the sunlight.

He could see Shelley trying to sidle towards the camera and away from the threat. She came up against the fridge, and stopped. She closed her eyes. The blade now rested on her nose. Even with the restricted view of a small screen, he could see clearly what was happening — and what was about to happen. She was totally helpless.

The man's voice came through the speakers. '*Sit on the floor!*'

He heard Shelley's terrified whimper. She stayed on her feet.

'*Sit on the fucking floor, bitch!*'

Her legs seemed to fold up beneath her.

'*Move and I will put this through your fucking skull. Do you understand me?*'

Twenty miles away, frozen to the spot, her husband could no longer see her. The intruder stood in his kitchen, pointing the axe downwards. Then he turned and looked straight at the phone.

'*Barry Lance. I know who you are. I know that every day you call your wife at this time. I know you are in your office at Langthorne House right now and I will know if you mention anything that has happened at your home to your colleagues. Do you understand?*'

Barry replayed the message in his mind. The voice wasn't familiar.

He bent towards the phone. 'You leave my wife alone.' It was all he could manage.

The man suddenly filled the screen. Then all Barry could see was black material. He had picked up the phone.

'*If you inform your colleagues I will kill your wife with an axe in her skull. If you do not follow my instructions to the letter I will kill your wife with an axe in her skull. Do not do anything stupid, Barry Lance. I am not blessed with patience or mercy.*'

Barry seized his phone. He had to hold it in both shaking hands. His jaw was clamped shut.

'I choose an axe. Not because it makes it easy, it doesn't. I choose an axe because it makes it fun. Do you understand? Or do I need to provide you with a live demonstration?'

'No! God no! What instructions? What do you want?' Barry held his breath.

'You can start by answering the phone.'

The picture disappeared, and the screen displayed *connection lost.* Barry stared at it. *What did he mean, answer the phone? Who was he? What just happened?*

He looked helplessly around his office, and then heard a shrill ring. He followed the sound upwards, to a black mobile phone taped roughly to the ceiling, vibrating with an incoming call. It was directly above the desk and Barry kicked over a lamp in his hurry to clamber up. He had to steady his hands as he picked at the tape.

'Yes?' Barry remained standing on his office desk.

'Good. You will need to follow my instructions if you want your wife to live.' The voice was clearer now.

'What instructions?'

'All in good time. Right now you have a meeting to go to. Put this phone in your pocket. I'll be speaking to you later in the day.'

The call ended and Barry stood looking at the phone. He ought to know how these things worked, he was a trained negotiator for God's sake. It was just that right now he couldn't remember what he had learnt, he wasn't thinking straight. He knew the man was giving himself time to move Shelley. He also knew that if the bastard was any good, it would be impossible to find her once he had done so.

And Barry was twenty miles away.

This man knew who he was, knew where he lived and who his wife was. And he'd managed to tape a fucking phone to the ceiling of his office. Barry had never been more on the back foot.

'Sir?'

Barry started. He hadn't heard the door open.

'Yeah?'

'Are you okay, sir?'

'Yeah, of course. Why?'

'Well, it's just that you're standing on your desk, sir. Is there a problem?' Barry was suddenly aware of what he must look like. His head almost touched the ceiling, tape hung down where he had just pulled the phone away. He had felt flecks fall onto his brow. They transferred to his hand as he wiped a layer of sweat away, it was white paint.

'I'm fine.'

'Are you going to the morning meeting, sir? I've been asked to come and get you. I think they've made a start already.'

'Oh.' Barry looked at the clock on his wall. He was never late for anything. 'Er, no, actually. Send my apologies.'

Barry climbed down from the table. He knocked a pen pot and a tray onto the floor as he did so but he did nothing to clear up the mess. His colleague stooped to pick up the papers Barry had scattered on his way out. The meeting room was to the right of his office. The way out of the building was in the opposite direction. Barry wheeled to the left and broke into a run.

Chapter 2

George Elms looked around and smiled. 'Nice place.' The Falcon Café was in the middle of the town of Gillingham, not far from the main football ground. It overlooked a large green, busy with people and their dogs. A man with a white apron emerged from behind the counter and greeted them with a big smile and an Italian accent. He swept past them carrying giant plates of fried breakfast. The sausages still hissed and bubbled. He gestured for them to find a table.

'First day out of prison means only the best.' Emily Ryker smiled back and led the way to a table in the middle of the room.

George stood with his hand on the back of the plastic chair. 'You wanna sit here? Not by the window?'

Emily shrugged. 'You can see out, can't you? We can move if you want.'

George looked around. A group of men occupied a four-seater table on the opposite side of the room, two of them flicking through the tabloids. They all wore jeans, work boots and matching navy polo shirts with a logo on the right breast — carpenters maybe, or painter-decorators. A family sat at another table. A young couple in a two-seater against the window looked to be nursing hangovers. Then a man sitting on his own, lost in a four-seater. He was hunched over a broadsheet, and barely moved.

'You may as well tell your friend to come straight over now. Otherwise he'll interrupt my meal.'

Emily looked puzzled for a few seconds. Her next smile was uneasy. 'It wasn't my idea.'

'Well, it certainly wasn't mine.'

Emily's chair scraped and she half stood. The waiter with the accent arrived at their table and greeted them.

'Just the two teas, please, for now,' she said.

'Two teas for you. You need more time for food?'

'No,' George cut in. 'I'm not sure if we're staying just yet.'

The waiter looked a little perplexed. He shrugged and nodded. 'Two teas.'

George watched Emily walk over to the man, still bent over the same page of his newspaper. She spoke into his ear, and he turned to take in George standing beside their table. He stood up and smiled. George didn't respond.

Emily was first back but it was the man who spoke. 'I'm impressed.'

George looked him up and down. He was tall, with broad shoulders and a neat, dark beard. He wore rimless glasses and a pinstriped shirt with cufflinks. His shirt was unbuttoned but he gave the impression that he might be more comfortable in a tie. George ignored the proffered hand. 'I'm not,' he said. He finally took a seat opposite Emily and glared at her.

'Emily didn't want to do this, George,' said the man. 'She warned me it was a bad idea. I had to practically order her.' He sat down next to Emily. He had brought his drink across, a tall glass holding the remnants of a black coffee.

He drank it just as the Italian arrived with their teas. 'Another?' He pointed at the tall glass.

Emily busied herself with stirring sugar into her tea.

'How did you know?'

George didn't reply. He continued to glare at Emily.

'I mean, just for the feedback really. I thought I was pretty good at the whole covert thing. I chose a good seat. I didn't even look up . . .' He petered out.

George looked at the man. 'Awful. You sat in the one seat no one would choose, right in the middle of the room. You had your back to the door. It's basic. You sit in a position where you can see everyone else, see your exits, see any attacks coming. And you didn't look up. Everyone else did, we all do, we all behave the same when we're acting natural. And Emily here didn't go for the two-seater by the window, which would have been the obvious choice.

'They told me you were very switched on. What makes you such an expert in human behaviour patterns?'

'Nine months in prison looking for changes in those patterns. Because that's when you know there's trouble coming. Basic survival.'

Emily interjected. 'Jesus, George. Don't be so fucking dramatic! This is Darren Lewis. He's assistant chief constable but he's effectively running the joint following recent events. He just wants to buy you breakfast and talk to you, that's all. You can listen or not. No one's here to make you do anything.'

'Anything to avoid paying, eh?' George shot a smile at Emily.

'And he's buying mine too.'

George turned to the ACC. 'What could you possibly want to talk to me about?'

'You're a sharp man, George, you've proven that already this morning. What do you think I want to talk to you about?'

'Oh I don't know. This cop killer problem you got? Or the fact that the highest ranking officer in the division appears to have been working with him and is now missing in action?'

'You're well informed.'

'You only need to pick up a paper. Your police service is a running joke.'

'It is. I have a lot of problems right now. And the biggest one is the ordinary coppers out on the street who need some direction from the ranks above them.'

'Are they not quite so trusting these days?'

'Who'd blame them? We've rolled from one disaster to another. Their colleagues and their mates getting wiped out, and then the most senior officer, after chasing the wrong man, goes and does a flit. And we still can't give them any answers about how Helen was involved. So you have hundreds of uniformed men and women sitting around making up their own stories.'

'And coppers do tend to believe the worst.'

'Of course they do. It's what we see all the time.'

'And they're probably right.'

'They might just be.'

George sat back. The Italian appeared. He placed a black coffee on the table and flipped his order book open.

Emily nodded at him. 'Three of your special breakfasts, please.'

'Any extras?'

Emily peered at her menu. The ones in front of George and the ACC were untouched. 'I don't think so, no. As they come.'

The waiter walked away.

George slurped at his tea. 'So. On the day I get released from prison, you go to the trouble of driving all the way up here to sit in a greasy café with me and Ryker. And what for? So you can tell me that no fucker trusts you? Is that it? It's not exactly a bolt from the blue.'

'I did go to some trouble to get here, it's true. I wanted to speak to you personally.'

'You want to know who you're chasing? And you think I must, seeing as how he picked me out as some sort of nemesis. Is that right? Well, I hate to disappoint you but this man, he ain't stupid. He knows that the case against me has folded because he meant for it to. He has people inside your force that are constantly feeding him information. And while he has that, he has total control over your environment. Total. I could tell you everything I know about him but it wouldn't cause him one iota of discomfort. Not one, because he wants you to find out. He controls what you know and when. You can chase him all you like but he'll always be three steps ahead of you.'

'You think that's *all* I want? For you to tell me what you know, then me and Emily here can go off and do some media appeals. Lean on some sources, maybe.'

'If you don't want that, what *do* you want from me?'

'I want you to deliver him to me, George.'

'I don't follow.'

'Maybe you're not as sharp as I thought you were. You're still a serving detective sergeant, right?'

'I am not.'

'Did you give your warrant back?'

George looked confused. 'No, I mean I'm still on the payroll but you people have been looking to get me out for over two years.'

'You want out?'

'Of course I fucking do. Once your employer nicks you, beats you and sends you to rot in a four-sided hell hole, the working relationship takes a bit of a hit. You know what I mean?'

'Yeah. I thought you'd say that. This is an opportunity though, George, for both of us. This fella is out there and he isn't finished yet, you agree with that at least. He left us a trail to follow and so far we've been merrily doing just that, but it's going to end with more officers dead. The area commander is missing in action, presumed to have some part in the whole thing, and is now wanted on conspiracy to murder — if she isn't dead herself by now.' Darren Lewis lowered his voice. 'I go into Langthorne nick and the whole place is full of shell-shocked coppers. I've never seen anything like it. It's not that there's a lack of loyalty. They just don't know whose orders to follow. They're like a pack of lost dogs down there, George.

'And you think I can help?'

'They'd follow you.'

George laughed. Too loudly. 'Don't be ridiculous! Last time I entered that nick every one of them wanted to tear me apart.'

'Well, now all they have is doubt. I see the way they look at me — they don't trust me. They're waiting to work out why I took on this job. The last two area commanders down there got involved with criminals for their personal gain. One's dead and the other's done a bunk. I need the officers to get together behind someone's'leadership. And the only person that has come out of all of this without any suspicion hanging over them is you.'

'I went to prison for murdering police officers. The crown offered no evidence against me and I was released. I've not been proven innocent. They just couldn't prove me guilty.'

'No one thinks you're guilty. They see you as a martyr, made to suffer while everyone else was getting away with it. I know it's quite a turnaround from a year ago, but you're the only one they'll follow.'

George laughed. 'So now everyone thinks I'm some sort of fucking hero!'

'No.' Emily butted in. 'You won't have everyone's support the moment you walk back in there. You'll have to work on a fair few people. But they will get behind you. They'll listen to you and do what you ask. As long as you are chasing this fucker that killed their mates. And going after Helen Webb. We all want answers from her.'

George looked at her. 'You think this is a good idea then, Ryker? You didn't just bring me here because you were ordered to?'

'I didn't think so at first. Just like you don't right now. But eat your breakfast, finish your tea and I'll drop you at your hotel so you can have a comfortable night's sleep for the first time in fuck knows how long. Then you can have a bit of a think about it. Who knows? You might just see that this isn't as stupid as it first sounds.'

George looked at Darren Lewis. 'What exactly would you want from me?'

'You come back to work as a DS, but your primary task will be to search for the man who murdered the chief and all those other officers. Then, when you have him, you can turn your attention to finding Helen Webb. If you want to, that is.'

'If I want to?'

'Yes. The cop killer is the most immediate threat to us. Helen Webb will turn up. I just thought you might want to be involved in making sure she does.'

'Is that why you've not put it out that Helen is wanted?'

'We will. The press will hammer us. They'll demand enquiries and resignations. All those things can happen later, but I can't have that circus going on while we're running a major investigation. I have a huge incident room running at headquarters looking for both, much has been done, but in nine months we haven't made any real headway. You can run independent, and from Langthorne House with a select few. You don't answer to the press or follow the structures of a Major Crime investigation, you only report to me. But I want our cop killer as a priority. Helen Webb is running away. My concern is the man who has been running straight at us. It cannot happen again.'

'And then?'

'Into the sunset with your full pension. If that's what you want. I'll write the agreement in blood if you need it.'

'Now who's being dramatic? So how's it going to work? I just walk back in, announce I'm back on the case and get someone to put the kettle on? You have to understand that I have some rather serious trust issues with some of our people.'

'You can choose your team. Keep it small. Be the only investigator for all I care. But some elements are already in place. Emily here will run intelligence gathering and Barry Lance is running the tactical side. He'll head any arrest teams, run any warrants—'

'Barry Lance?'

'Yes.'

'He and his team are the ones responsible for dragging me out of my car and beating me in the street. I have no intention of standing in the same room as that man ever again, let alone working with him. Or anyone from Lennockshire Police, come to that. This is a bad idea.' George sat back.

'We can talk about Barry. Emily's right, we should give you some space. I would have liked to have given you a bit of time before meeting you and giving you my pitch, but time is not a luxury we have at the moment. I know you'll understand that, at least.'

They fell silent. Darren Lewis seemed to come to a decision. He stood up, scraping his chair. A business card dropped onto the table in front of George.

'It's a stock card. I don't have one of my own. But I've written my contact details on the back. Call me with any questions.' Darren paused. George didn't look up. 'Or with any answers.'

Darren tossed two twenties on the table. Clearly not a man who frequented breakfast cafés.

And then he was gone.

George looked at the phone number. He flipped the card over and snorted at the tagline. *'Lennockshire Police: protecting those who cannot protect themselves.'*

The waiter arrived with three plates. George smiled and indicated for him to put the third plate down. 'It'll get eaten, don't worry.' He pointed at the forty quid. 'And keep the change.'

* * *

Barry Lance leant against the slab of teak that crowned their kitchen island. It was all Shelley had wanted — a damned island. It had taken the removal of a load-bearing wall and the installation of two steel struts to make it possible. Barry still wasn't sure of the overall cost. His wife had even insisted on new plates and cutlery to go with it. Suddenly the old stuff just wouldn't do.

He went first to the cupboard where they kept Shelley's medication. There was a lot of it. She had chemotherapy medicines that fought the disease and other drugs to fight the side-effects. These made her sick so she took more drugs to lessen the nausea and still others to prevent her kidneys or liver giving out. The doctors had assured him that the only way to deal with something as aggressive as cancer was to match that aggression, and more. The doctor had smirked at this point and told Barry that being a police officer, he should understand this.

Barry didn't think that was funny.

All the medication was still there, even the painkillers. The bastard hadn't taken any of it. Barry searched the rest of the house. There was nothing out of place, nothing disturbed, nothing taken. Apart from his wife.

Barry's phone rang, making him jump. He saw the ACC's name on the screen. Barry's first instinct was to ignore it. But then, if anyone had the power to help him it might just be Darren Lewis.

'Boss?'

'Barry, I just got out of the meeting with George.'

'Okay.'

'Okay? That's all you have to say? Don't you have any questions?'

'It's not for me to ask questions, boss.'

'You still don't think this a good idea, do you, Barry?'

'Is he in?'

'I don't know, to be honest. I really don't know. You may well get your wish, Barry, and he'll walk off into the sunset.'

'Or you get yours and he ends up involved in the most important investigation we've ever had.'

'Well, when you put it like that . . .'

'Are you sure he's right to be back, boss?'

'No, to be honest. But there's no one else who can do it.'

'You still think he's going to flush our man out?'

'Our man's got unfinished business. He'll come for him again, especially if we build George up as the returning hero.'

'And make him the prime target for our cop killer.'

'As long as he's shooting at George Elms, he's visible. And he's not shooting at anyone else. He wants George, so we need to make him accessible.'

'I'm still not convinced of his innocence, boss. Where there's smoke, sir. . . and George is made of it.'

'We just need to manage him while he's useful to us, which could be a very short time.'

'It's going to piss people off. A lot of the others won't see the returning hero thing at all.'

'I get that. It's a gamble, and George isn't going to be easy to work with. He's not exactly in a trusting mood.'

'The feeling's mutual.'

'The official investigation continues from headquarters, nothing's changed there, I said I'd do everything in my power to find this man. George Elms is just another option. Look, we'll talk more when I know more about George's decision. In twenty-four hours this could all be academic, anyway.'

'Is that how long you gave him?'

'We didn't talk about that, but George won't be hanging around when it comes to deciding about his future.'

'I see.'

'Are you sure you're okay, Barry? If you need to say something, I'm all ears. I want you to be as candid as possible about this. I know it's a gamble.'

'I'm fine. I'll do what I can to make it work.'

'I appreciate that. We'll speak soon.'

Barry threw his phone onto the teak. He hadn't dared mention his situation. As long as only he knew what was going on, his wife would remain unharmed. As soon as he told someone else, he risked losing control. Barry didn't know anyone he trusted enough for that. He exhaled loudly, and his eyes went to the chalkboard hanging on their kitchen door. They often used it to exchange romantic messages. Now it was covered in someone else's scrawl.

Nothing Stupid Now.

Chapter 3

Finally she appeared from between two cars, with her head down. She had a bag over her shoulder, the strap gripped tight. She was on her own.

Fuck! She was on her own.

George looked out across The Leas. He was at the end furthest from the town centre. There was a wide stretch of grass between the bench he sat on and his wife, who was walking slowly towards him. He desperately wanted their daughter to be sprinting behind her in the late summer sun, her mousy hair catching its rays. But she was alone. She was looking at the ground, her arms by her sides, definitely not keeping an eye on any mischievous child.

George turned from her to face the sea. 'Be calm,' he muttered to himself. 'You never know.' She might be just around the corner, sitting in McDonalds with the in-laws. It was mid-afternoon, the quiet time of day between lunch and dog walking. The benches were occupied by Langthorne's retired, come to enjoy the elevated view of the English Channel.

'Hey!' His wife was calling to him.

George swallowed. He pretended to be surprised, and stood up. Their embrace was stiff. Neither of them seemed to know how to act.

'How have you been?' George said.

'Good.'

'It is so good to see you, Sarah. It feels like a lifetime.'

'It does.'

'You look great.'

They sat down, Sarah on the edge of the bench, her hands together in her lap. 'You've lost weight,' she said.

'You don't tend to eat too well where I've been.'

'I'm sure you don't.' There was a silence.

'I was really hoping to see Charley. I thought that was the agreement.'

'I know, I guessed you were. I'm sorry I didn't bring her. It's been really hard on her, you know. I didn't want to bring her out here and think everything's all right again when, well . . . it isn't.'

'Does she even know I'm out?'

'No. I haven't figured out what to say yet. I'm waiting for the right moment.' She wouldn't look at him.

'But everything is clear now, isn't it? I got acquitted and released. What more are we waiting for?'

'We've been here before, George. We thought everything was good, that it was all over, and look what happened! I just need to be sure. We both need to be, so we don't cause that girl any more distress.'

'You mean, so *I* don't cause her any more distress.'

'Take it how you like. She idolises you. You're her dad, of course she does. But how was I supposed to explain why you had to go to prison?'

'I know it must have been hard.'

She shook her head. 'You don't know. You can't.'

'It wasn't a walk in the park for me either, Sarah.'

Sarah spun round and faced him. 'But you put yourself there, and you stayed! I spoke to your solicitor any number of times at the start and it was pretty clear that you could have ended it any time you wanted. They only kept you there because you said you did it. Why?'

'I did it for you. For you and Charley. Do you think I wanted to be in there? But I knew you were safe while I was in prison.'

'Why didn't you tell me that?'

'Because you're bloody-minded and viciously intelligent and if I'd told you just a little, you would have made it your job to find out the rest. And that would have put you in real danger.'

Sarah sniffed. They looked away from each other, out at the view.

'And what about now?' she said.

'Now I don't know.'

'So that explains the message about me *disappearing*.'

'Yes.'

'Do you have any idea how difficult that is with a seven-year-old girl? With *our* seven-year-old girl? I can't keep dragging her out of school, moving her from house to house on vague bits of information, just because you keep assuring me that we're in danger. You need to tell me what's going on.'

'I can't. Not until I've had a bit of time to find out for sure.'

'At least tell me what you do know. What is this big threat and why can't I even trust the coppers to protect me?'

'You can't trust anyone, you have to believe me on that. I will tell you everything, I promise. I just need a bit of time to get it all straight.' He looked down at his hands.

'Here we are again. That's all I hear from you, George. You started off telling me that it's all over, you're out of prison, acquitted, and I should be telling our daughter all about how it's all back to normal. And now you tell me that you need time to get it straight, whatever *it* is! Life is never normal with you, George. That is the only certainty that's come out of these last two years. All I want for Charley is a normal life.' Sarah got to her feet.

George looked up at her. 'I need to see her, Sarah. I need to be with you both. We can be a family.'

'Not a family, George. You may be happy to live your life on the run, but I'm not, especially when you won't even tell me what we're running from. I am going to disappear, just like you told me to, and no one will find me or Charley — not this mysterious threat, not Lennockshire Police and not you, George.'

'Just sit and talk a bit more. I can sort this.'

'No, George. You remember that night when we brought Charley home from the hospital for the first time? When she was so small she couldn't get her hand round your little finger? You promised me that we would never grow up, that we'd stay young and silly and carefree for Charley, with none of the problems that eat other people up. Look at us now, George, look at our daughter. Who knows what damage we've done to her in the last two years, the damage *you've* done!'

Sarah walked away. George stood up and took a step after her. Then he stopped, and his hands dropped to his side.

'We can still have that life, Sarah!' he called out, his vision blurred by tears.

'Not with you. You've put an end to that life.'

Sarah didn't look back.

George let her go. There was nothing he could say that would make anything better. He would find her and they would be a family again. He would just have to make it safe first.

Then once and for all they could stop being grown-ups.

Chapter 4

Mick leant on his shovel. The man he knew only as the Irishman, or 'Irish' for short, dropped to his knees beside him, taking the weight of the grey, pitted patio slab that was next to be manoeuvred into place. Two other men were looking on. Mick picked up the hose, aimed it into the cement mixer, and span it to clear out the leftovers. Then he brought it to a halt.

The sudden silence was beautiful.

'Fuck me, she's a noisy old beast!'

'Reminds me of your mum.'

Mick cast his eyes over their handiwork. 'We should finish the whole slabs today,' he said to no one in particular. 'Then just back in the morning for the last bits, a few cuts. Couple of hours maybe.' No one replied.

Mick and Irish walked out to the front drive. Their work van was parked awkwardly, hanging over the lip of the drive. The men had stashed their lunches in the back, hoping it would remain in shade. Mick heaved the large metal door open, and Irish leant in. Mick noticed something move past the front of the van.

It was a car, a black Volvo estate. The passenger side of the car was closest to the van. The man sitting inside wore sunglasses and he was staring at the van, the number plate in particular. Mick thought he might have been writing it down. Irish had reached into the van to grab his lunch bag, but stopped and looked up at Mick. They both watched the Volvo, which had stopped just fifty metres away. It was a quiet area, the neat bungalows mostly occupied by retirees. The Volvo turned. It picked up speed, came back past the van and took a left out of the estate. Both men watched it go without comment.

Mick took his own lunch and they walked back to the rear of the house, careful to put their feet on the ornate stepping-stones across the lawn. The two other men were laughing, taking the piss out of each other. The laughter stopped when they saw the Irishman's face.

'The cops were out the front. They were watching us,' Irish said.

Mick shrugged. 'It's no biggie, boys. We're just a gang of ground workers with a job on. It's the whole reason we do this shit.'

'They must know, though. They must know about the job.' Ainsley was the youngest of the crew, just eighteen, black, dreadlocked, and solidly built.

'They don't know nothing,' Mick said. He ran a dusty hand over the stubble on his head.

'Then why the fuck are they sat out there watching us work?' said Ainsley.

'They just know we're active, or they think we might be. They wanted us to see them. They were letting us know that they're watching so we *don't* do anything.'

Ainsley looked at him. 'How come you know so much?'

'It's what I would do if I was a copper.'

'Maybe you missed your calling, Mick!' The Irishman laughed. 'Do we need to change anything though, man? I mean, seeing the law this close to a job, it ain't good, is it?'

Mick shook his head. 'No, we don't need to change nothing. We just need to be careful, yeah? Boys, those fools practically stalled their car in front of me. Listen, we're just a gang, out doing our job, so let's shut up and eat. We get it done, we get paid and then at the weekend we get *paid*!'

The four men laughed. Ainsley whooped.

'Ah, fuck!' Mick was digging around in his lunchbox. 'Anyone need anything at the van? I forgot my water.'

Mick walked back to the van. The street was empty, save for a silver-haired gent six houses away battling with a bright orange lawnmower. Mick heaved at the side door and leant in, looking back to make sure none of the crew had followed him. His thumb moved fast over the keys on his phone.

Gotta lv this weather man. U fancy a beer anytime soon? Enough to make you thirsty.

He sent the message to someone listed only as T. Mick burrowed in the van for the water and the reply soon popped up.

You know me, I'm always good for a beer. As long as it's not Fosters again. Felt shit for days!

Mick checked again. He was still alone.

Fosters it is! Round 8.

* * *

Eighteen miles away in the town of Langthorne, intelligence officer Emily Ryker sent her text to the undercover officer and made her way back to her desk. At eight o'clock tonight she would access one of the email accounts used by her and her asset, who was currently infiltrating a crew of thieves who specialised in high value cash break-ins. *Fosters* was the code word indicating which email account she would use. She would read a message saved to drafts, delete it and save her response in the same box. They made as little contact as possible, so there must be a problem.

Chapter 5

The jeep slithered on the stones, mud, and metal shards of the approach road to Alcani's scrap-metal yard. Helen Webb had to fight to stay on course. It had just got dark. The car bucked through a deep gulley and as it rose back up, Helen was relieved to see its headlights pick out a slate-grey metal gate. She bought the jeep to a stop several metres short of it.

Helen knew more about Alcani's yard than most of the people who worked there. A web of mug shots featuring various Alcanis had been decorating the wall at Langthorne House police station for some time. One of the area's largest organised-crime groups (OCGs to Helen's old colleagues), the Alcanis ran their operation out of this site. Career criminals, the Alcanis were now into their third generation after immigrating from Albania. Since most of the second generation were now in prison, Sol Alcani, the son of Nial Alcani — the most senior mobster to be sent down — now sat at the head of the family table. Following a raid on the premises, fourteen of them had been convicted, but for money laundering rather than the murder charges or weapons-supply jobs that she had been hoping for. Helen had wanted to join that raid but hadn't been able to. She could never have foreseen that she would one day be counting her lucky stars that she had missed it.

The Alcani family weren't finished. They were too big for that. Lennockshire Police coppiced the family tree when they took Nial out, but it soon grew three more heads. The family were still involved in everything from crude and petty burglaries right up to moving weapons, large amounts of drugs and organising killers for hire. But now they were probably more careful.

Helen Webb switched off the engine and stepped out of the jeep. The headlights still pointed at the gate. It was eight-foot tall, made of matt-finish steel and locked firm into magnetic housing topped by barbed wire. The gate was new, doubtless put up in response to the raid. The police wouldn't breach this one.

Helen crossed her arms and leant on the bonnet of the car. There was no buzzer system, and no point shouting or flashing. She was certain her presence had been noted by the state-of-the-art movement-detection and CCTV systems hidden among the trees. And from the less subtle camera that overhung the gate like a giant desk lamp.

Helen waited.

After nearly twenty minutes she was just starting to feel the temperature dropping when she saw movement. A man sloped towards her and coughed on a cigarette. He'd probably lost the argument over who would go out. He was obviously trying too hard to be casual, and walked far too slowly.

'We're shut,' he said.

'So I see.'

The man's fingers poked through the mesh on the gate and he looked her up and down. 'So fuck off.'

'You talk to everyone like that?' Helen stepped up to the gate.

'I'll talk better tomorrow at eight. When we're open.'

'I didn't come here to speak to you.'

'No one else here, love. I suggest you come back in the morning, like everyone else has to.' The man turned away, already digging in his pocket for another smoke.

'Sol Alcani will want to speak to me.'

'I don't know who that is,' the man called out. He didn't slow his pace, didn't turn his head.

'He knows who I am. Tell him Helen Webb is here.'

The man disappeared out of sight.

Helen waited some more.

Another twenty minutes. Then the gate made a noise, or rather it didn't. The electric hum was suddenly gone. The gate shuddered, then slid open, and an orange light flashed. She stayed where she was until the gate had opened fully. She looked straight ahead. Twenty metres of rutted track which then twisted away into an area of woodland. The site itself was hidden from view.

'Seems like we are open after all,' the smoker called from the darkness, 'but I don't reckon you've got long.'

If anything, the road on the other side of the gate was even worse. The left turn had a high camber where the big trucks with their heavy loads of metal had worn away the surface as they turned. The jeep was old. It was the first car she could get with the cash she had hastily withdrawn before the police could freeze her accounts. It had cost her £450. She had left her BMW in a residential street in Maidstone. Needs must. And those same needs now had her jolting up to a Portakabin, the only building on the site with any sign of life.

She climbed out of the jeep. The windows of the Portakabin were brightly lit. She could hear people moving about inside, but it was raised on stilts and she couldn't see in. She took a quick look around the site. Two silhouettes dominated the skyline — directly ahead of her was the huge warehouse that she had seen in photos of the raid and, on her right was a huge pile of twisted scrap metal, one of the means for laundering their dirty money.

The man from the gate had already walked in, letting the door close behind him. Helen made her way up the steps, into the bright room.

'It really is!' He was seated at an ancient plastic table. Sol Alcani. Helen recognised him from the photos. Three other men were at another table close to the wall.

'Helen Webb,' he said, and nodded.

Helen couldn't have known what response her name would prompt, if any. She hadn't been able to think of anything else to say. She had expected to be on every news channel by now. The press would have eaten up her story — her betrayal, her possible involvement in the deaths of officers, of the chief no less. But there hadn't been a word. Helen guessed why. Lennockshire Police was a PR disaster and had been for nearly three years now. It couldn't let this story break too, not yet.

'It really is,' Helen said. She managed an uncertain smile. The man facing her looked dishevelled. He was in his late thirties, of medium build. He was wearing woollen shorts, a battered grey hoodie and pit boots. His English carried a slight accent.

'My people tell me you are not a very popular lady at the moment. Or you're *very* popular indeed, depending on how you look at it.'

'I guess you could say that both are true.'

'Way I understand it, your police friends would be very interested to know where you are right now. There might even be a reward. Is there a reward?'

'Not yet.'

Sol smiled. 'So I should keep you here until there is one, should I?'

'I'm here to offer *you* a reward, something no one else can.'

'Oh really?' Sol sat up straighter. 'I'm interested.'

'I need to disappear for a while. I need some things I reckon you can get for me, some ID documents, maybe even a bolt hole where I can buy myself a little time. And I need money.'

Sol looked puzzled. 'You want my *help*?'

'Yes.'

'I was interested. I mean, you sparked my curiosity, so I opened the gate to see what was going on. I did not expect you to walk in here and ask for my help. Your organisation and I don't get along, Helen Webb. Why would I help you out?'

'I want to strike a deal.'

Sol jerked forward and spat. 'I don't deal with fucking snakes. The last time your snakes came here they took away my family. They fabricated the evidence, made up lies and sent us down. I don't see that as grounds for a fucking deal, do you?'

'I'm not part of that anymore.'

'Oh, so that puts us in the same team now, does it? How do I know this isn't all bullshit? Who says you're not strapped up with technical right now, and my voice is being transmitted back to your fucking pig mates? Maybe this is how you weasel your way back in — a punishment posting.' Sol shook his head. He nodded at the gate man.

'Search her. Search her good.'

The man turned to Helen, grinning. He ran his eyes down her baggy jumper, over her tight-fitting black leggings to her brown, fur-topped boots. She was in good shape, looking younger than her age with her shorter hair, now dark red.

'Take off your clothes,' Sol called out. The lad looked back over his shoulder and smiled at his boss.

'I'm not taking anything off.'

'Take off your fucking clothes,' Sol replied. The boy's smile widened.

'Every relationship has to have an element of trust, doesn't it, Helen? Right now you've got some making up to do. I need to be sure you've got nothing on you. Now *take off your fucking clothes.'*

Helen weighed up her options. One of the men had moved towards the door, blocking it. They all stared at her intently. She reached under her jumper and pulled out an A4 envelope that she had been holding flat against her body. She stepped forward, and threw it on the desk in front of Sol.

'That—' Helen began.

'Take off your fucking clothes!' Sol lashed out at the envelope, and it span off the table. He rose to his feet, his chest rising and falling, and stood with his hands flat on the table. 'We don't say another word until I know you are not recording this conversation.'

Helen stiffened, then raised her jumper and pulled it over her head.

'No wire,' she said.

'You haven't been searched yet.' Sol nodded at the lad, who stepped forward with his eyes on her chest. Helen looked up at the ceiling while he ran his fingers across her belly and up towards her breasts. Looking straight at her he put his hand inside her bra and took hold of her nipple. Then he put his hands behind her back, as if they were hugging. She averted her face from the cigarette stench on his breath. Her bra slipped down to her waist.

Sol Alcani laughed. 'This has to be done properly, Helen.'

She said nothing. The lad moved round behind her and pushed against her buttocks, clearly aroused. His hands moved down her sides, then forward. His fingers pushed under her waistband and then beneath her underwear.

Helen's elbow shot back. The blow connected with the lad's nose and he bent double. He was spouting blood even before he hit the floor.

Sol Alcani laughed again, and slapped the table. 'Fuck, I didn't think he would get that far!' Helen dragged her jumper back over her head, while the lad at her feet squirmed.

'You done with your games?' Helen snarled.

Sol turned his attention to the envelope on the floor, and he gestured at one of the older men, who picked it up and handed it over. 'What is this?'

'Your old man and all the rest. They were convicted on the evidence of four undercover officers and two informants from within your organisation.'

'That's not news. Your lot came here with a confident swagger. It didn't take a genius to put two and two together.'

'I'm sure. I was responsible for what happened to them after they'd served their purpose. Those papers give the name of one of the men who supplied us with information. He still works for you. He isn't on our payroll anymore.'

Sol held up the envelope and shook it. 'That's in here?'

'Yes. You get another name when you give me some ID I can travel with. I give you the rest in exchange for a safe house until I can leave the country with £500,000 clean cash.'

'Five hundred grand! And a passport! What makes you think this so-called information is worth that sort of money?'

'I don't *think* anything. I know it is.' Helen looked at him.

'And you're just going to give me the names of your colleagues? You know what that means for them, right?'

'I'm selling you information. Whatever you do with it is down to you.'

'Jesus. That's proper cold.'

Sol nodded to one of the other men, who leafed through the contents of the envelope. The man then walked towards the door, still holding the papers. He kicked the lad as he walked past him.

'Get up, you fucking idiot, there's work to be done.' The lad scrambled to his feet.

'Do we have a deal?' Helen kept her eyes on the man still seated in front of her.

'We'll see how this one goes. I need to be sure you're not giving me duff information. In the meantime, I have a place you can stay, right out in the woods, perfect for what you need. I'll have someone take you there.'

Helen shook her head. 'I have a few things to sort. I will be back in touch in a few days. I need to be away from here, this place gets a lot of attention. It's the last place I want to be seen.'

Sol smiled. 'Stay here for the night then. Your only chance of getting away clean is to blend in with the traffic during the day.'

Helen nodded. He was right. Moving after dark she would be more visible.

'Fine. I leave tomorrow after you open.'

Sol nodded at the remaining man, who beckoned to Helen. He led the way out of the room and back down the steps.

'We'll need to take a car,' he said, tugging at the door of a parked Isuzu truck.

Helen turned towards her Jeep. 'I'll follow you down.'

'In this one.' The man held the passenger door open. Helen knew it would be pointless to argue. She was in their hands.

* * *

Sol Alcani watched the rear lights of the truck disappear and put his phone to his ear.

'Yeah?'

'It is her.'

'Okay. What have we got?'

'She's got information for us. The cunts who brought us down.'

'All of them?'

'Possibly. She's drip-feeding us. She needs some things in return, money mainly.' The man on the other end was silent for a few moments.

'We need what she has.'

'I agree.'

'She doesn't get a penny though. I suggest we ask her again, but this time we can be a little more persuasive. She might be playing us.'

'My thoughts exactly.' Another silence.

'This seem right to you though? I mean, she's playing a risky game coming here, talking to us. She must know that we don't have to play ball.'

'She's desperate. Trust me, I saw it first-hand. She's run out of options.'

'She must be desperate. Where is she now?'

'I'm putting her in the rat run. I can't have her getting nicked. But don't worry, she won't be leaving.'

'Did she give us anything yet?'

'A name. I'm sorting it.'

'You do that.'

Chapter 6

At the front counter of Langthorne House, the two middle-aged women were almost hidden behind a high desk. They both wore *Police Support Staff* badges stitched to their breast pockets. One busied herself at a computer terminal, and the other was leaning on the desk, going through some paperwork with a man who seemed out of breath.

George Elms stood in front of the seated woman. It took her a while to raise her eyes, and then she started.

'Oh, hello.'

'Hello, Joan.'

'Jane,' she corrected him, looking even more uncomfortable.

'Close.' George shrugged. 'I wanted to speak to Darren Lewis.'

'Will he be expecting you?'

George grinned. 'I don't think he'll be surprised.'

Jane picked up her phone. 'Hello, sir, sorry to bother you. Are you still on station at Langhorne House? Only I have a gentleman down at the front counter who has asked to speak to you. He says you're expecting him.'

George shifted his weight from one foot to the other. The other woman, whose customer had stomped off, was now staring at him.

'It is, yes. Okay, sir, I will let him know.' Jane put down the phone.

'He *was* expecting me then?' George said.

'Someone will be down shortly to collect you.'

George sat down to wait. He had wondered what it would be like, walking into the place after all this time, and on his own terms. He had thought he would still be angry. He was even worried that he wouldn't be able to control it. Or that he'd be nervous, conscious of his former colleagues' reactions. But he sat staring at the posters and messages scattered across the wall, feeling nothing. Nothing at all.

Someone pushed at the door through to the main station. Barry Lance stretched out a size-twelve boot to wedge it open.

'George,' he said. 'We need to go see the boss.'

* * *

George walked a few paces behind Barry, who ushered him into a conference room. Emily Ryker, was waiting for him at the long boardroom table.

'Ryker.' George nodded and sat down facing her.

Darren Lewis arrived carrying a tray of hot drinks. Emily and Barry stood when he entered. George stayed where he was.

A sharp-featured woman bustled in behind Darren, found a seat at the end of the table and readied a notebook and pen.

The boss set down the tray. 'I'm told you like your tea, George. Thanks for coming in.'

'I'm just here to tell you what I know. I can give you someone to chase, but I can't promise I'll be around for anything more than that.'

Darren took a seat and leant forward on his elbows. 'Well, okay then, it'll be a start.'

George nodded towards the unknown woman. 'Who's that?'

'Lisa Jones,' she said. 'I'm the intel DCI. I was in the north of the county, working closely with your friend Detective Constable Ryker here as a matter of fact. Mr Lewis asked me to come down and lead the intelligence for this operation.

'You vouch for her?' George said to Emily.

'Yeah, if that still means anything to you.'

George ignored the dig, accepted the sentiment. If Ryker trusted her, it was at least something.

'So what can you tell us, George?'

'Nothing without tea.' George poured five teas, took one for himself and held it in both hands. The others waited.

'The man you are looking for is called Kane Forley. He's changed his name though, his surname at least. He did tell me what it was but I forget it now. It was a stressful time . . .' The image of his friend, Sam, came into his mind. Her curly blonde hair was plastered to her forehead, and she was trussed to a chair with her eyes wide in terror. She was pleading with him not to kill her. 'Kane won't be known to you — us. He isn't on any system, never been nicked, never had his DNA taken and he knows that gives him power. We're chasing someone who doesn't exist. His DNA and fingerprints match no one.'

'He's been sloppy, though.' Darren Lewis was suddenly full of himself. 'We got DNA hits from a number of the scenes. He practically left us a trail when he abandoned his bike on a towpath in Hythe so we could pin him to an area, and then ditched his helmet practically outside the address where he murdered Ed Kavski. We've been left with all the pieces for a very simple puzzle.'

'He's not sloppy.' George looked straight at the boss. 'Whatever you've found, it's because he wanted you to. It's all part of what he's trying to do. He thrives on control and on fear. Think about it. We attend a murder scene, find DNA and we've won, right? It's all we need. But Kane knows that this has led us nowhere. We still don't have him in our custody, in our control.'

'We know who he is, though,' Darren said.

'Doesn't matter. Kane Forley knows that I've been released and he'll expect me to talk to you. He's very clever, and we are very predictable. Us cops have standard operating procedures for just about every incident, and guess what? They're all readily available if you just know where to look.'

'So he's clued up on how the police work and he's using that to avoid us?'

'He's using that to taunt us. He's rubbing it in our faces. The man's doing pretty much what he wants. He shot the chief of police dead, for fuck's sake. In broad daylight, and then he disappeared.'

'So how do we find him?'

'We don't.'

Darren shook his head. 'You must have a better answer than that, George. I came to you because I thought you might be the one to bring him in. Are you telling me you can't?'

'No one can. Whatever he's planning, it will happen soon. Sure I could find him, given enough time, but he knows that.'

'So we just wait? And for what? More police deaths?'

'We need to be less predictable. He wouldn't expect me to come back here, and we can use that.'

'Shit!' Barry Lance got to his feet suddenly, waving a vibrating mobile phone. 'I have to take this!'

The spell was broken. 'Now?' said Darren. 'You need to take it right *now?'*

'Yeah. Five minutes and I'm back.'

Darren waved his hand. 'We'll carry on.'

* * *

Barry ran down the corridor and answered the call.

'Don't leave me fucking waiting again, Barry, or I'll get angry. I get very fucking careless when I'm angry.'

'I couldn't help it.' Barry was almost encouraging, just like he had been trained to be. 'Let's be calm. I had to get out of a room full of people.'

'Other people don't matter right now, Barry. There's no one more important in your tiny little world than me. Do you understand?'

'Of course I do. Now, please, how's my wife?' Barry felt suddenly weak, and his hand shook. But he knew what to do. Stay calm.

'She's safe, Barry. And she will stay safe as long as you do what you're told, understand? Your wife says you're good at doing what you're told.'

'I'll do whatever you need. I just don't want anyone to get hurt. Tell me what you need.'

'Well, I must say I am liking your attitude, Barry. George Elms was a lot less cooperative.'

'George Elms?' Barry's voice shook slightly. The man had confirmed his worst fear. 'Kane,' he said. A mistake, but he couldn't help it. His wife was in the hands of Kane Forley, a man who had already killed indiscriminately, and who sought total control over his prey. Barry knew that was exactly what he was.

Kane chuckled loudly. 'Seems I've earned myself a reputation over at Langthorne House! I assume that's where you are. And George Elms has told you all about me, has he?'

'I know you're angry, Kane. I'm starting to understand why. It must have been so hard—'

'Don't you fucking dare! Don't you fucking *dare* try to talk to me like that!' Kane lowered his voice. 'I'm not some attention-seeking fucking kid standing on a cliff edge, Barry. Don't try talking *me* down. I'm no amateur. I killed your colleagues, Barry, and you need to help me with the next stage or I am going to cut your wife into pieces. Do you understand *that*?'

Barry's voice was breaking now. 'I was just trying to—'

'Don't. Don't try and do anything other than what I say. No one gets to know about our situation, *no one.* If I get even a sniff that you're talking about it, I will use someone else, and that means you and your wife are no longer any use to me. And I don't need to spell out what that means. You don't fucking talk *me* down.'

The call ended. Barry put his hand on the wall, and lowered his head.

It took him a few minutes to regain his strength. He stared at the phone. He knew he had to go back to the meeting or someone would come looking for him. He walked in, mumbled an apology and sat down.

* * *

George was in full flow, and barely noticed Barry. He was talking about Kane's family, and particularly Kane's brother. George had been part of one of the interview teams when Will Forley was first brought in for sexual offences.

Will Forley liked children, especially girls aged between five and thirteen. His interest in them had escalated to the point where sharing images on the internet was no longer enough. Detective Constable Samantha Roberts had led the interview. Will sat still, his head down and his hands in his lap. Sam asked him the standard questions. She ended by asking for his computer passwords and Wi-Fi code, and whether anyone else had access to his property. Will responded to every question with a terse *no comment.* Eventually Sam sat back and looked at George. He took it as a sign to change tack.

Are you sexually attracted to children, William?

George liked to be direct. He would make the interviewee uncomfortable in order to provoke a reaction, even a negative one.

Are you going to be able to control those urges? Or are we just waiting until you rape a child, Will? And then maybe you'll kill her to hide what you did? Should we lock you up now, Will? Make the world safer?

George had been in no mood to mess about. He'd hardly given Will time to answer. He knew he wouldn't. A scared, middle-aged man ripped out of his comfort zone and facing two angry coppers was only ever going to follow the instructions of his legal advisor.

Tell me, Will. What sort of a man sits there, accused of these terrible things and says nothing to defend himself? I'll tell you this, Will, it isn't an innocent man. An innocent man is outraged, appalled. An innocent man can't wait to tell me how wrong we are.

George left a long pause. The pauses were every bit as important as the questions, even more so.

But to tell the truth, admit you're guilty? To say out loud what you are, maybe even for the first time? That takes bravery, a bit of backbone. You don't have that, do you, Will?

The legal advisor cut in, and told George that he was bullying his client into an admission. The weasel. Of course George was bullying him. That was how you got to the truth. Back then, George had been naïve enough to think that the truth mattered.

He wasn't sure now.

Darren brought him back to the present. 'So we know plenty about his brother, but nothing about Kane. Where's his brother now? Can we get to him, see if he will help us out?'

George shook his head. 'Dead. His mum too. That's what kicked this whole thing off. Will Forley served a short sentence and was then released on conditions, and I found him breaching those conditions. He was hanging round outside a school — my daughter's school. I put him back in prison and he hung himself soon after. His mum took it badly. The story got out, and she suddenly became the centre of a lot of unwanted attention. She did the same thing, hung herself in the bedroom Will had occupied for most of his life. A terrible story really, a whole family suddenly gone. Except for Kane.'

'So he blames you?' asked Darren.

'Me, Lennockshire Police, the chief constable. Everyone but his brother. It's become an obsession. He wanted to hurt me. He said he wanted to give me the same choice his brother faced, to go to prison as a marked man or to take my own life. He got part of his wish, but it clearly wasn't enough. I'm still here.' George gave a wry smile.

'And the chief? Why him?'

'It wasn't about him personally. It was about the organisation. He blames us all for hounding his family, for making their lives a misery, and for not doing enough to protect his mother. She pretty much suffered in silence. There were some fairly unpleasant incidents, but I don't think she called us once. She had windows smashed, her car defaced, she was spat at and assaulted in the street. Kane holds us all responsible for it.'

Darren looked grim. 'Not a man to be reasoned with, then.'

George shook his head. 'He never was. He wanted Lennockshire Police to be afraid for their lives, every man and woman wearing that uniform or in the offices back here. He was pretty damned successful too. He's highly intelligent. He can interpret patterns of behaviour and manipulate them to his advantage. That's how he set me up. He knew you would take the easy way out, and you did.'

'So how do we catch a man like that?' asked Darren.

'His behaviour has escalated,' said George. 'He progressed from shooting a young lad and an elderly PCSO to taking out a sergeant on a bike. Then, on police premises, he hit the detective sergeant who was in charge of the investigation. That was much more of a challenge.'

'Then he did away with the chief constable himself,' added Darren.

George nodded. 'In broad daylight, at an official function. It's true that Helen Webb assisted with that one, but we don't know exactly how. We do know that he relies on information that's leaked to him, and Helen isn't the only source.'

Darren looked shocked. 'You think he's still getting information from someone within Lennockshire Police?'

'He'll have a plan B,' said George. 'Who's to say it wasn't him behind Helen's vanishing act? She could be part of it. But I'm certain there's a plan. He'll be back.'

'So where do we start?' Darren looked helpless.

'The first thing I need is a team I can work with, and this bloke won't be included.' George gestured at Barry, who had been staring at the table since his return. Now he looked up.

'Well, that's not your choice,' Darren said quickly.

'It is, or I walk.'

Barry looked at George, his expression hard. 'What? Because my team were a bit fucking rough when you got nicked? Tell me you wouldn't have done the same! I should have put a fucking bullet in you, and then maybe this prick would have left us alone a long time ago.'

George and Barry stared at each other, and then George nodded. 'At last, some honesty.'

'I've not been anything but honest. I don't think you should be in this building at all, let alone this office. You may not have done what you went to jail for but you're not innocent, George Elms. A lot of people were killed or badly hurt, just for being close to you.' Barry shook his head.

'You're angry because you didn't have the balls to finish me when you had the chance.'

'You certainly were pathetic, I'll say that. It would have been like shooting a lame horse. And you're not much different now.'

'Barry! George! Please!' Darren banged on the table and stood up. The two men remained locked in an intense stare. 'Great! The very two people who might be able to find him and stop him are at each other's throats! Well, stop it. Kane Forley is out there right now, a free man. George, you said yourself that he's a manipulator. Don't you think this is exactly what he would want?'

'I need people I can trust.' George's eyes were still fixed on Barry.

'I don't need him,' Barry shot back.

'I need you both. This force needs you, or more of us are going to die.'

George looked away. He stood up, hesitated, then walked towards the door. He pulled it open and stopped. 'More of us *are* going to die, there's no doubt about that. This is already damage limitation.'

The door closed behind him.

* * *

'What are you going to do to me?' Shelley asked. It had taken her some time to pluck up the courage to speak. The man seemed to be beside himself with rage. He was facing away from her, leaning against the wall of the trailer. She knew he was calling her husband. He had said she could speak to him, but then he became angry and cut the call.

She repeated her question.

He lit a cigarette and turned to face her. 'Your husband needs to understand who I am, and what I am capable of.' His mouth was flecked with spots of saliva and his eyes flashed.

Shelley took a step back. 'What are you going to do to him?'

'If he helps me, and does as I say, nothing. You will both get your worthless lives back.'

Shelley raised her head. 'What's that smell?'

'Weed. You want some?' Kane seemed calmer now.

Shelley shook her head. 'Not that. I mean the smell in here.'

Kane smiled. His anger seemed to dissipate as abruptly as it had flared. 'No idea.'

'There's something rotten.'

'Could be anything. These trailers carry all kinds of foodstuffs.' He shrugged.

Shelley could see very little from the trailer. She had been brought here in the back of a van with no windows. When she was finally bundled out she had caught a glimpse of a huge warehouse covered with thick creepers. He led her to the rear of an HGV lorry trailer, whose door was already swinging open. It was furnished with a small mattress, a sleeping bag and a few pots. A beer barrel stood in the middle, serving as a table. They must be near a main road. She heard the incessant roar of fast-moving traffic close to where they were.

'Sure you don't want some?' Kane held out the joint.

'No. Not that stuff.'

'It keeps me calm. Stops me doing things I might regret.' Kane took a long drag and blew the smoke into her face. Shelley's headscarf had come a little loose, it hung low on her forehead. He reached out and pulled the side to adjust it. She recoiled.

'You hate me, don't you?' He looked pleased. 'Don't worry, Shelley. This doesn't end well for me.'

Kane laughed, and then he stepped down into the dust outside. Still chuckling, he slammed the rear doors shut.

1.

Chapter 7

The door was easy. An amateur could have slipped it, and he was no amateur. The man looked back along the dark street to make sure he was unobserved and rolled his lock-pick kit back up in its soft bag. He pushed the door open and stepped into the porch. There was a second door, dimly illuminated by the street light outside. This one had no locks. He pushed it open and walked in.

Nice place. Neat and tidy. Muted, earthy colours on the walls. He reached out a gloved hand and switched on a lamp that stood on a small wooden table. It gave off a warm glow. The man looked at the many photographs arranged in a neat pattern on one of the walls. Two people stared back — evidently a happy couple holidaying in different places, goofing around with hats and sunglasses, and in one picture a monkey. No kids — as per the brief. Time to get to work.

The man walked on. To one side, the stairs. On the other a short hallway led to the kitchen and then an open-plan dining area at the rear of the house. The living room was at the front, off the same hall and the room closest to where the man stood. He pushed off his slip-on shoes. The wood flooring felt solid and expensive. He was wearing dark, tight-fitting trousers and a long-sleeved top. He slipped on a white paper suit and pulled the hood taut across his forehead. He adjusted his surgical face mask so that it covered his mouth and nose, and captured his DNA before it could leave his body.

He opened the door to a cupboard under the stairs. It held the standard hoover, coats and some shoes. Plenty big enough for what he needed. At the back, attached to the wall, he noted the fuse box. He shut the cupboard. He walked along the hall, through the kitchen to the back door, counting the steps as he went. There was a key in the lock. He turned it and opened the door. Nodding to himself, he locked it again and then returned to the hallway to switch off the lamp. He practised the walk until he was able to do it blind. He switched the lamp back on while he unzipped his suit in order to pull his Glock 23 handgun from its underarm holster. He screwed on the silencer.

He turned his attention back to the cupboard. He entered and crouched inside, getting as comfortable as he could in the small space and making sure none of the contents touched him. He didn't want to shed any DNA. Then he pulled the door shut, and the light of the lamp shone through the gap under the door. He felt for the meter box, and the biggest switch that must control the main fuse.

He pushed it down and the darkness was complete.

Chapter 8

Emily Ryker was reluctant to move from the patio, and its view of the sea. She'd been transferred to the southernmost tip of the county from its northernmost point. When it became apparent that it was not going to be the 'temporary' stay she had been promised, she found a tenant for her place in Gravesend and looked for a house on the south coast. Suddenly she was able to afford something a bit more special, and the place she found was certainly that. From the front it was an ordinary terraced house on a main route from Langthorne through to Hythe. But the rear was a different world altogether. All the houses had a fifteen-metre patio that finished at the promenade. For Emily, moving to live near the sea had been a silver lining. She had never imagined that she would end up living right on its pebbly doorstep.

She sighed and got to her feet. In the kitchen, she scooped up her laptop, refilled her gin and tonic and hurried back to the patio. She had the place to herself. None of the neighbours were sitting out, even on a warm night like this. The moon brushed a gleaming pathway over the sea. Perfect.

The computer screen was too harsh in the dark. She opened up an email account and found a new message in drafts.

Hey,

We got some attention on us today. You know what that's about? This job goes down tomorrow night. I'm leading the crew now. This job goes right and I'm a step closer to the real work. I can't have this go wrong — can you assist with keeping it clear?

M

Emily rolled her eyes. It was either those idiots from Organised Crime swinging their dicks and trying to give the impression that they knew what they were up to, or else some senior intel bod had got wind of a job and wanted to put the frighteners out. She would sort it tomorrow. She deleted the message and typed out a new one.

Nothing to do with me. It'll probably just be a couple of bored intel drones. I'll sort it. Any updates of interest?

She saved her message as a draft and logged out. It took ages to have a conversation but it was safe. She and Mick were the only people aware of the login for the email account and nothing was ever sent or received, so nothing could be intercepted.

Emily took a long swig of her drink. Her gaze drifted back to the moon, then to the blinking boats that made their way slowly across her field of vision. Her mobile rang and she swore at it. This was not destined to be a relaxing evening.

'George. I'd like to say this is a pleasant surprise.'

'Bad time?'

'Yes.'

'You can still talk, or you wouldn't have answered.'

'Just tell me how come you called at all, having been such an arsehole recently.'

'Okay. Well, maybe I called to apologise.'

'Did you?'

'No.'

'You've got sixty seconds, then I'll find better things to do.'

'Look, Ryker, you should have told me you were taking me to see that Lewis fella. I don't like being duped. I've had enough of being led up garden paths, and I was really gutted that it was you holding my hand this time.'

'Listen to yourself, Elms. When did you get so full of shit? I thought it was for the best. Or at least I thought you'd appreciate knowing your options.'

'Well, now I do.'

'So? What? You called me to have a pop at me?'

'No! Fuck no. I wouldn't have mentioned it. That's not why I called, Ryker.'

'So that's an apology of sorts.' She picked up her glass and put it back down again.

'Not really.'

'I'll take it anyway.'

'I called about my wife. She was part of our agreement, remember? You were supposed to be protecting her.'

Emily sighed. 'I'm not your personal intel officer, George. I told you I would do what I could. And let's not forget that you ducked out of seeing your wife on the day of your release. You say you're being duped? Well, what about your wife?'

'You'll be happy to know that she hates me.'

'That doesn't make me happy. The sooner you sort your shit out, the sooner you can stop looking at me with those hungry eyes.'

Emily laughed, despite herself.

George chuckled. 'Well, I'm not made of wood, Ryker.'

'Makes sense. So what do you want from me? I already told you I helped her get lost. No one from Lennockshire Police is going to find her. I gave her a crash course on how to stay off the grid and how to be careful.

She's a smart girl, George. I think she intended to disappear anyway.'

'But you know where she is?'

'What do you mean?' Emily looked longingly at her glass.

'What I say. You must know where she is!'

'No! I spent forty minutes of our lives teaching her how to make sure coppers like me can't find her. I'm good at it. It's what I do. There would be very little point in me doing all that and then walking her to her door, would there?'

'But I need to know where she is.'

'Why don't you just ask her, George? She's your wife.'

'You're still pissed with me.'

'I'm pissed with this whole situation. I'm not your personal go-between. My job doesn't include making sure your wife is kept safe, George. I don't want to be the one to blame if that doesn't happen. That isn't fair! Anyway, you haven't been straight with me about what the danger is.'

'She just needs to be disappeared. From anyone who might look for her.'

'Like you, you mean?'

'Everyone except me.'

'Well, you need to start making yourself clearer, George. She's gone, and she won't be found unless she wants to be. Or she fucks up, and this threat that you are so obsessed with turns out to be real.'

'It's real, Ryker.'

'I've done my bit, George. And you've had your minute.'

Emily heard George sigh. 'I am sorry, Ryker — that I pissed you off, I mean. You've been good to me, too good really. I owe you a gin and tonic.'

Emily smiled into the phone. She could never stay mad at him for long, and it annoyed her. 'Nah. I don't touch that shit anymore.'

George chuckled. 'Oh I see. So you're sitting with a cup of tea, are you?'

'You can fuck off now, George Elms.'

She put the phone down, still smiling. She logged back into the email account. Sure enough, her draft message had been replaced.

I thought the same.

Nothing at the moment, but it'll be on Sunday afternoon 1600. After this job I may need your assistance with smoothing the way. I need this to be clean.

She deleted the message and made a mental note of the time. These days she wrote nothing down. She drained the rest of her drink and considered another. She wanted to be relatively fresh for the day ahead. Lord knows what might happen, now that George Elms was around. Well, whatever went down, she was happy to have him back.

Chapter 9

Crouched in the cupboard under the stairs, he heard someone open the front door. Just short of two hours. Well, he'd waited longer than that in the past. The man shifted onto one knee, resting the other foot against the wall. He heard two voices, a man and a woman. The woman was giggling. There was a click. One of them had tried a light switch.

Nothing.

'Ah shit.' It was the male voice.

'Power cut?'

'The neighbours had lights.'

He heard a footstep outside the cupboard and readied the weapon.

'Must be a fuse.'

The man licked his lips in anticipation. This was the best part — the moment just before. A beam of light appeared underneath the door, and the handle turned.

He fired twice, with a sound like compressed air. The mobile phone jerked out of his victim's hand and landed with its light pointing upwards into the face of a wide-eyed woman standing at the door. Another flash, then the sound of a second body falling to the ground.

He didn't have to wait long for the silence. There were some scuffing sounds, shoes against the wooden flooring, but they soon ceased. He reached a gloved hand to the switchboard, and the scene was floodlit.

The man emerged and stretched. He took his time, avoiding the blood. He switched off the light and followed the steps he'd practised earlier. He opened the back door. The air outside took his breath away after the stuffy cupboard. He walked to a high boundary wall and looked around. None of the neighbours had stirred. He removed his paper suit and pushed it into a bag taken from one of his pockets. He locked the back door and slid the key under the *Welcome* mat.

Another clean job.

Chapter 10

Blue and White's café was named after the racing colours of a local celebrity biker. His parents had owned it for as long as anyone could remember, they had changed the name when his first trophy had gone up on display. On a Saturday mid-morning it was busy.

Three blokes occupied one of the tables. The fourth returned, frowning, and sat down in front of his half-eaten breakfast. He took a swig of tea. You could always tell when the Irishman was pissed off.

'Wassup?' asked Ainsley.

'I just spoke to the other crew.'

'There a problem?' Mick swallowed a mouthful of food.

'They're one down.'

'For tonight?'

'Forever.'

Ainsley shook his head. 'What happened, man?'

'They got sent a message is what happened. One of them was working for the law.'

'Who?' Mick barked.

'They didn't say who, just that they're one down. They didn't really want to speak, you know. It ain't a good time over there.'

'What does this mean for tonight? I mean it's fucked, ain't it?' Ainsley said.

The Irishman shrugged. 'I can't see how we can carry on with it. If this fella's been talking to the pigs, he must have told them about the fucking job tonight.'

'We don't know that,' Mick said.

'We don't know nothing. That's the problem. You always said we should leave nothing to chance. Well, this is a big fucking chance.'

'Did they speak to the boss?'

'They tried. Anyhow, they know we're out grafting tonight,' said the Irishman.

'Yeah, and they haven't told us to put it on ice, have they? The last thing they need is seven of their blokes nicked. If they thought that was possible, they would be telling us, wouldn't they? I say we're still in the clear.'

'You want us to crack on? One of their crew gets found to be a rat and you want us to carry on with a job that he knew everything about? That's fucking stupid, man.'

'Jesus, Irish, give it a rest. We'll finish up here and I'll make a call in the van, away from ears. I'll see where we are.'

They finished their breakfast in silence.

* * *

Danesh Alcani.

Everyone's right-hand man, or so he would have you believe. No one trusted cousin Danesh, but he behaved like he was in charge of the whole operation. He was a pain in the arse. He had been given the job of point of contact for the crews out doing the less subtle stuff — the dirty jobs.

It kept people like Mick from bothering the boss and made Danesh feel important.

'This had better be good, man,' said Danesh. We're up to our necks in shit over here.'

'You having a bad day?'

'What do you want, Mick?'

Mick hated the way Danesh pronounced his name as 'Meek.' 'I need to make sure we're all cool for tonight. I hear you flushed out a rat in another crew. Well, that particular rat knew all about our activities.'

'We've sent a message. Listen, it's shit from the past, nothing about what's happening now. You're in the clear for tonight.'

'You're sure? You're saying he's not been speaking to them recently? This job's been on the cards for—'

'Fuck it, Mick! What did I just say? So long as you don't fuck up, you got a free run tonight, no problems. I expect a call tomorrow, with some fucking numbers.' Danesh ended the call.

'I bet you do,' said Mick to the phone. The others were all watching him. 'The man was flushed out for some old shit. I didn't get much else, and I got the impression we don't need to know. But tonight is on.'

'Have you spoken to the other crew? See if they've got the same idea?'

Mick shook his head. 'I'll call, but the word from the Alcanis was pretty clear. This job happens tonight, whatever.'

Chapter 11

George stood, hesitant, at the door of a bungalow in Temple Ewell, a village just outside the port town of Dover. George checked his scrap of paper one last time to ensure he had the right door for Paul Baern's house. It matched with the image he had in his mind. Certainly George could see why Paul used to enthuse so much about walking his Labrador in the valley to the rear. George wasn't sure how Paul would react to him. He needn't have worried. He received a one-armed hug.

'George! Fuck, it's good to see you.'

'Paul!' A shrill voice called from inside the house.

Paul grimaced. 'Got the grandkid today, forgot my language.'

George laughed.

'It isn't easy, you know. Come in!'

George followed Paul inside. The house had large windows in the lounge and kitchen so the light flooded into every inch.

'Tea?'

'Obviously.' A woman stood a little further in. She wasn't smiling. 'Hello, George.'

'Karen!' George pecked her on the cheek. She didn't move.

'You want tea, love?' asked Paul.

'I'll have a coffee,' she said, still looking at George. 'You got out then?'

'Yup. Legally. I mean, there's no need to call the police or anything.'

'A lot of good that would do. They don't seem to know their arses from their elbows, that lot.' Karen snorted. 'They'd be sure to bang up the wrong bloke right?'

George nodded, feeling awkward. 'This is true.'

'You want to sit in the garden?' Paul asked.

There was the sound of something breaking in the living room, and Karen turned away. George and Paul went out onto a patio, and the famous dog-walking valley opened up in front of them.

George sat facing the view. 'Where's the Lab?' He regretted the question as soon as he'd asked. There could only be one answer.

'We lost him, mate. Cancer.'

'I'm sorry about that.'

'Yeah, so were we. He was one of the best.'

George changed the subject. 'Grandkids though!'

'Yeah. Harry's three now.'

'Jesus. I remember you conning me for time off when he was born.'

'I know. Seems like only yesterday, doesn't it?'

'I dunno about that. Seems like a fucking lifetime to me, mate.' George turned his face to the sun and closed his eyes.

Paul stood up. 'I'll just go finish the tea.'

A whispered conversation took place inside the house that George did his best to ignore. He could guess what it was about. He was suddenly aware that he'd outstayed his welcome, but his tea arrived piping hot.

'Listen, Paul. I didn't just come round for a catch-up, you know. I was hoping to talk shop.'

Paul grinned like he missed shop. 'What do you need?'

'What's your status there now, Paul? I've been hearing all sorts of things. One person even said you were dead! I mean is there any truth in it? Are you dead, first of all?'

'They could be right there. I do like a lie-in.'

'You are retired then?' George asked.

'I wish! There was an incident with our friend Helen Webb. I found out some stuff around her — you know the details, I'm sure. I hadn't been happy about her for a while, and sure enough I was right, like I always am. Anyways, she got the hump and decided to pick on the disabled.'

'I hear she knocked you out clean with one punch.'

'That woman can hit!' The two men chuckled. 'After that, the senior bods realised they needed to do something with me, and none of it involved police work. I've been surplus to requirements for some time, but at least they're doing something about it now. I'm on gardening leave. They're finalising a deal to get me out on medical grounds. I should get my full pension, though I think the lump sum might take a hit. I can still find work. I'm not completely fucking useless.'

'Not completely. How is the arm?' George pointed at the place where he had fired a bullet into his best friend. It was his final act before their careers and their lives took a nosedive. George had been terrified, backed into a corner and reacted to what he perceived to be a threat to his own life. But it had been Paul coming through that bedsit door, his expression of concern immediately distorting to pain. It was a moment neither of them would ever forget.

'It's better. I don't wear the strap so much anymore, and the involuntary salute has all but stopped. Now it just hangs there limp and useless. The wife says it suits me.'

The bullet had struck Paul in the shoulder. According to the movies, a person can take it in the shoulder in the morning and be stitched up and back to saving the world by afternoon. This is far from the truth. Paul never fully recovered. The bullet hit bone, which splintered. Part of it collapsed his lung and almost killed him. Another piece tore through the nerves controlling his arm. Paul would never be able to use it again.

They were silent for a while, and then George brought up the reason for his visit. 'So you're ready for the quiet life then, are you? Away from the job, I mean. What do you see yourself doing?'

'Well, she ain't gonna let me retire!' Paul jabbed his thumb back towards the house.

'I don't see that suiting you anyway.'

Paul shrugged. 'True. But I like a bit of fishing. I intend on getting another dog, I think. You know, once I move on a bit from my old Lab.'

'I understand.'

'And you? Lennockshire Police's worst nightmare come back to haunt them.' Paul grinned.

'Like a bad smell, you mean? Well, get this. I walked out of prison straight into a meeting with Darren Lewis.' Paul looked blank. 'The assistant chief constable?'

'Oh, right. Never heard of the man. I'm not very good with ranks. I assume he was trying to talk you out of suing his ass?'

'Not exactly. I actually don't think he would be too bothered if I did, just as long as I helped them out a bit first.'

'They want your help?'

'They've got it, Paul. I'm back at Langthorne House, leading the search for the fucker who took Sam out, and all those others. And I'm after Helen Webb too. She's going to answer for what she did.'

'Fuck off!'

'Paul!' Karen's voice shrilled from the lounge, but Paul ignored it this time.

‘I swear. I went back to Langthorne House yesterday morning, messed around a little, found the kettle. I’ve even considered hooking out the old tea Frisbee. You remember that? If you catch it, you make it.’

‘Fuck off!’

‘Paul! Jesus!’ This time there was real anger in Karen’s voice.

‘Let’s not use the Lord’s name in vain, honey!’ Paul called out.

George shook his head. ‘Don’t, please. She’s already upset at seeing me.’

Paul smiled. ‘Yeah, you’re not her favourite person. But if you tried to get her to say why, I think she would struggle. She’s just pissed at the situation.’

‘Well, that and the fact that I shot you.’

‘That’s the situation I’m talking about. By now we all understand what happened and why. It was a fucker, and now look at us. Me a registered cripple and you the returning hero, sitting in my back garden and begging me to come back and save the day. Just like it ought to be!’

‘Who said anything about begging?’ A smile crept over George’s face.

‘Well, asking then.’

‘I was getting to it.’

‘You want me in tomorrow?’

‘Hell no! Tomorrow’s Sunday. You can start Monday.’

Paul narrowed his eyes. ‘Are you in tomorrow?’

‘Of course. But then, what else have I got to do? You’ve got your family, mate. You’ve also got a pretty difficult conversation to have with the good lady in there.’

Paul leant back and turned his face to the sun. ‘She is good too. We bicker, you know, but it’s because we care about each other.’

‘Of course it is. How will she take it, do you think? Will she be keen for you to get back to work?’

‘I haven’t said yes yet, have I?’

‘Alright then. Say no.’

Paul grinned. 'Yes.'

'Without checking with the boss? Brave man.' George smiled back.

Paul's eyes were closed. 'I remember when I was in the hospital with the head injury, courtesy of that witch, Helen Webb. It really wasn't serious. Well, the wife stormed into my room and said I was never going back. The people I worked with couldn't be trusted, and it was going to get me killed. She was so upset.'

'I can imagine. She might have been right too, Paul. It's not exactly been good to you, mate.'

'True. So anyway, we both agreed that I should call it quits. My work was kinda done by that time. I had played my part, I'd exposed what I needed to and the witch had made a run for it. It was game on, but it was up to the younger, fitter officers to chase her shadow. I couldn't help with that bit. So, me and the wife lived on top of each other for a week, and then she couldn't wait to get me out of the house and into some kind of job. She'll object at first, but it won't be such a hard sell.'

'You're up for chasing shadows again, then?' George looked at him.

'I always was, mate, so long as I've got the right people next to me.'

'Excellent. Well, if you don't mind, I'm going to get the hell out of here before your wife starts objecting.'

Paul shook his hand. His left arm flapped at his side.

'Good shout.'

Chapter 12

The atmosphere in the van was thick with tension. Mick was in his usual place at the front, with the Irishman driving and the other two seated in the back. Mick was in charge of two crews tonight. They had met in in the car park of a deserted garden centre just outside Langthorne, and then gone their separate ways.

Mick's crew was headed for a cluster of garages near the railway line, about three hundred metres from Langthorne West train station. The garages were rented out to anyone who could afford them. Mick had decided that it was the perfect place to start from. Their van bore plates 'borrowed' from a Network Rail vehicle. Mick reckoned this would fool any police patrol on night duty in the vicinity as long as they didn't go beyond cursory checks.

The other crew was in a saloon car. By now they should have dropped the woman off at the prearranged spot.

It was two in the morning and the crew was growing restless.

Mick had been staring at the signal scanner for a full ten minutes and the lights still hadn't flickered. It was a simple device, a small black box with lights that came on when the receiver detected a police radio broadcast in the area. It was available on the internet, entirely legal and invaluable to a crew of crooks waiting for the best time to get to work.

That time was now.

Mick tapped at his phone. 'You all set up?'

'Yeah, we're good.' The other crew was ready on the opposite side of town.

'Anything?'

'Nah, the air's dead, we had a flicker a few minutes ago. I reckon they're all a-fucking-sleep, lazy cunts. You want me to wake them up?'

'Yeah. Let's get this done.'

* * *

The man dropped the cheap Nokia phone back under the armrest and opened the car door. They were on a one-way street with a large expanse of parkland to one side and a defunct hospital on the other. A group of kids had gathered in the park, waiting. The lead boy was sitting on his bike, smoking a cigarette. The man went over to him.

'We're good,' said the boy, and the man handed him a bundle of tenners. He returned to the car and watched the stream of kids — about twenty of them — cross the road and make their way towards a row of terraced houses.

The kids followed their instructions to the letter. From a nearby building site, they gathered bricks and rocks and began throwing them at the parked cars and then the houses. The road was under siege. Soon the sound of alarms tore through the night air. When it reached a crescendo, the kids ran back through the park into an alleyway, where they could starburst in different directions and make good their escape.

The box lit up in a frenzy of flashing lights, and the two men monitoring it shared a chuckle. Every available police resource in the area would be woken up, and turned out of their sleeping holes. Diverted.

Time to move.

* * *

She was almost invisible in the long shadows cast by four enormous excavators. The machines had been shifting thousands of tonnes of pebbles along Sandgate's beach to reinforce the sea defences. She answered her vibrating phone, gave a one-word confirmation and walked out into the harsh floodlights. She picked out her favourite excavator and climbed up into the cab. In less than half a minute the row of spotlights mounted in front turned towards the surrounding fence, and the beast burst out of its enclosure. She turned right and headed into Langthorne. She checked her watch. Her ETA was eight minutes.

* * *

'Eight minutes, men. Time to move.'

Mick and two of his companions jumped out of the van. They wore high visibility jackets with *Network Rail* written across the back. The Irishman stayed in the van. They scrambled up a muddy incline to the fence that stood along the railway line. They made short work of the wire mesh and returned to the van, where they picked up their kit for the next part of the operation. Each of them pulled a balaclava over his face and Mick led them in a jog back up the slippery slope and onto the rail track. Mick carried an axe and a wrecking bar, and the other two hauled the steel rope and grappling hook.

Five minutes had passed. The platform of Langthorne West train station was dimly lit. The giant clock above it marked the seconds with a clack. There was no other sound. The trains and their passengers were all in bed.

Mick scrambled onto the platform and readied his axe. The brick building housing a small café and the public toilets also offered a grey metal cash machine sunk into its wall. The screen flickered a warning in neon green. *Be aware of your surroundings, criminals may be operating in this area.* Mick struck the first blow. The axe dug into the brick wall by the top left corner of the machine, where the metal lip met the brick. He pulled it back to take another swing.

* * *

The excavator roared past the darkened van and the Irishman within. The wall of lights at its front jerked upwards as its tracks hit the bank. The diesel engine bellowed and the beast broke through the steel fence posts as if they were drinking-straws. It came to a stop at the top of the bank and Mick watched the woman emerge and slide down the bank to where the Irishman had the van facing forward. A chain trailed from the excavator, and the Irishman hooked this to the front bumper of the van. The woman ran back up the bank, revved the metal beast and the van jolted forward. The excavator dragged the van up to the railway line, where Mick and the others were waiting.

* * *

Four of the excavator's grappling hooks bit into the partially exposed ATM machine. The brick wall surrounding the ATM shuddered, and then crumbled away. The adverts still rolled across the screen as the digger ripped the machine from its housing and the ATM slammed onto the platform, sparking and smoking from its exposed wires.

The bucket rose, dangling the ATM high above them. The woman skilfully lowered it over the van and spun it to face the rear doors. Mick jumped into the back and fastened the ATM with ropes as the digger lowered it towards the van's flat bed.

It was done. The van reversed back down the track, leaving the excavator where it stood, halfway across a track that would be busy with commuters in just a few hours' time. The crew and the woman operator piled into the front of the van and they made good their escape.

* * *

Mick waited for the woman to disappear into the night before he made the call to the gatehouse at Alcani's yard. The warehouse behind the steel gate would provide the perfect location for the next stage — what was known in the business as the 'kill site'.

* * *

Just as the police filed the final report of criminal damage to vehicles and houses in the area of Radnor Park, Langthorne, the distinctive noise of a diamond-edged disc cutter against toughened steel filled the interior of the Alcanis' largest warehouse.

Chapter 13

Sipping a takeaway coffee, George Elms walked up to the second floor, where he had been allocated a space to work from.

'What's going on?' he asked.

Emily Ryker looked tense. 'There's been a shooting.'

George looked at her, waiting for more. It didn't come. 'That all you know?'

'Top end of Hythe. Some fella and his wife shot dead in their home. Looks like a pro hit.'

'You think it's linked to our thing?'

She shrugged. 'No idea.'

'Okay. You're stressed about it though. Who's the victim?'

'According to Major Crime it's some bloke that might have links to the Alcanis.'

'Oh. For a minute I thought it was something important. It'll be some drug debt or internal feud then. Is the kettle on yet? Only I've nearly finished this.' George raised his cup and started towards the kitchen.

'George!' George heard the urgency in Emily's voice, and stopped. 'Can I talk to you?' she asked.

George gestured towards a vacant office and they went in. 'What's going on, Ryker?'

'This shooting last night.'

'Yeah?'

'He used to be a source.'

'For us?'

'Yes, for us.' Emily sounded impatient. George still wasn't following.

'Okay . . . But we still don't think this is linked to our thing?'

'No. Not to our thing, but it might be linked to *my* thing.' Emily stared at him.

'You have a thing?' George was really puzzled now.

She looked down. 'I run sources.'

'Were you running him?'

'No.'

'No as in *no*, or no as in *not officially*?'

'No as in *not at all*. I've never had any dealings with the bloke.'

'Ryker, it's been a while. I'm a little rusty. You're obviously worried, I just can't see why.'

'I *am* running a source that's close to this fella. They work together. The dead guy used to be a source, my guy still is.'

'And is he dead?'

'No, he was working last night.'

'Sounds to me like your dead guy fucked up and got dead as a result. It happens. Your man needs to be careful, but that ain't gonna be news to him if he's ratting on the Alcanis for his wage.'

'He's a warranted constable for his wage.' Emily looked grim.

George put his coffee down. 'Oh, so he's not a source, he's UC?'

She nodded. 'My guy is, yeah.'

'You're running undercover officers now too?'

'I shouldn't be. They gave me some of the UC stuff after Helen went, because I'm kind of an outsider. They bought Lisa down to oversee intel as a whole.'

'Lisa?'

'Yeah. She was in our meeting yesterday — the DCI.'

'Okay. We like her, right?' George was still frowning.

'I don't like her. She's far too fucking attractive to be likeable. But she's good and she can be trusted. I get the feeling they suspect this leak is coming from intel.'

'It could be anyone,' said George.

'I know.'

'So you're worried about your officer. I can understand that. Does he know any more about what happened with the dead guy?'

'And his wife.'

'And his wife? Jesus, poor cow.'

'I don't know, I haven't had a chance to speak to him yet. I'll be making contact in a couple of hours at an internet café in town. You wanna come along? I know you like good company with good coffee.' Emily gestured at his cup.

'Sure. Nothing more exciting is going on here, and at least I can be sure of some good coffee.'

Emily nudged him playfully. She was in mid-nudge when the door opened. They both jumped.

'Sorry!'

The woman spoke with an Eastern European accent, and George recognised the cleaner. She had been there every morning for as long as he could remember. She drew back and shut the door.

'I don't like her either.' Emily jerked her thumb at the door.

'Is this a racist thing?' George teased.

'No!' Emily laughed. 'Too attractive.'

Chapter 14

Helen Webb woke to the sound of someone hammering on the caravan door. She was still in her clothes, having decided against the filthy mattress in the bedroom area. She had finally managed an uneasy sleep on a sofa.

The man who had done the knocking was a new face to Helen. When she opened the door, he turned and walked in silence towards a waiting Land Rover Defender.

Helen called after him. 'Can you take me back to my car? I need to be getting away now.'

The man continued walking. Helen looked out, squinting in the bright sunlight that flickered through the trees surrounding the caravan. Tucked underneath them, it would be invisible from the air. She reckoned it wasn't too far from the northern perimeter of the yard.

The man opened the Land Rover's passenger door and made his way round to the driver's side. Helen checked her watch. It was 6.30 a.m. She walked through the grass towards the vehicle, her shins saturated with dew.

She looked at the driver. 'Do you have any water?'

'No,' he grunted. He had muscular arms and shoulders, but his belly protruded. His head was shaven and there was stubble on his chin. He wore a stained sleeveless vest, revealing a *Betty Boop* tattoo on a bicep and *Only God Can Judge Me* etched along the top of his chest like a necklace.

'Are you taking me to my car?'

'No.'

Helen sniffed. She knew she had made a serious error in coming here.

The Defender bumped its way back to the main site. To her right, the giant warehouse loomed — it looked far larger in the daylight. Helen knew that behind it was a three-metre-high fence and beyond that an old farmhouse that was home to the younger Alcani brothers. The Alcanis owned numerous properties, and Sol could be living in any of them.

They drove into the hushed interior of the warehouse. It was a vast, open-plan area, almost as big as a hangar. It was filled with cars in various stages of dismemberment. The Defender rolled to a halt and the driver jumped out. The door closed so hard that the vehicle rocked on its ageing suspension. He strolled towards a series of partitioned cubicles that evidently served as offices, and entered one of them.

Helen scrabbled for the door handle. To her surprise, the door opened. She climbed down and shut it behind her. The sound reverberated through the building. Helen ran through her options. According to the aerial photographs, the perimeter fence should be just beyond the wall facing her. If she could get to it she might be able to find a way of climbing over and onto the main road.

Then what?

Helen had forgotten that there was no longer a life for her out there. She was a convict, on the run and without a car. Or was she? Among the lines of cars awaiting destruction Helen spotted a Suzuki Vitara, hers. It looked to be in working order. She patted her jumper pocket, and the keys rattled. She could avoid the main gate. There were other ways out of this site, although she didn't know where they were. But if she could get mobile, follow the tracks around the site, maybe she would stumble across an exit before they found her.

The car was about fifty metres from her. Helen bent forward and sprinted. She made it to the car and found it unlocked. She stooped to get in and stopped dead.

The roof lining hung down, almost touching the steering wheel. It had been slashed along the length of the car, from front to back. The central armrest had been ripped out and lay where the rear bench seat had been. The two front seats had also been slashed, and they bled their sponge stuffing into the foot-wells. The dashboard sat at an angle. It had evidently been ripped out and then hastily pushed back in. Helen gritted her teeth, pushed the key into the ignition and turned it. The little jeep didn't even make a noise. Now Helen knew for certain that they were not going to let her leave.

'What can I say, Helen? We tend to be a bit careless when we're looking for something.' Helen gasped.

Sol Alcani turned away and was heading towards the Defender. 'Did I scare you?' he called back.

'You made me jump.'

'Why don't you come over here and talk to me?'

Helen saw the silhouettes of two other men beside the parked 4x4. One man leant on the back of a chair. The second was fiddling with a lamp that he positioned facing towards it. Then they all looked at Helen.

'That chair for me?'

'Who else?' Sol Alcani didn't look back.

'I don't need to sit in a chair to speak to you. Anyway, I've done all my talking for now.'

'I don't think so. We have more to talk about.'

She remained where she was. 'Not like this.'

'Come and sit in the chair, Helen. I'm done shouting.'

'Not like this!' Helen raised her voice.

Sol Alcani erupted. 'Sit in the fucking chair!'

Helen closed her eyes and her body sagged. She was all out of options. She moved forward like an automaton.

Sol put out his hand and invited her to sit.

'Now we can talk.'

* * *

Mick peered into a rusting mirror that clung to the wall above a basin. He was trying to wash away the fine metal filings that had flown out while they were dissecting the ATM. His arms and chest ached. It had taken more than three hours to carry out the operation, which had to be undertaken with surgical precision in order to preserve its precious cargo. This ATM was an older model. Most modern cash machines were primed to release an ink that would mark the cash and render it worthless if the machine was tampered with.

Mick had been patient. He and the Irishman had taken their time, aware that one wrong move would render their pay-out worthless. Cash does that. It has a way of focusing the mind.

Mick looked like shit. He had had no sleep for nearly twenty-four hours and was pale and exhausted, damned near dead on his feet. But his work was done. For now.

He turned away from his reflection and made his way back to the parked van. 'Not a bad night in all, boys.' He rubbed his hands together.

The Irishman smiled. 'We've had worse.' Ainsley whooped from the back. Mick wound down his window for some fresh air, and saw a figure lit up by a spotlight sitting on a chair and facing a stationary Land Rover Defender.

'What the fuck's going on over there?'

'I don't know,' said the Irishman. 'I see Sol Alcani himself is running the show, so it ain't something we got any business involving ourselves in.'

Mick peered out. 'Fuck that, we just earned them a cut of ninety grand! Drive a bit closer at least.'

'You trying to get us fucking killed?' But the Irishman needed to pass the spot to get to the gate. Mick squinted at the seated figure, and at Sol Alcani, who was standing with one foot up on the Defender's bumper. Mick watched a thickset man approach the chair, dragging a heavy, steel chain.

The Irishman pulled away. 'You see anything? You see who it was?'

Mick shook his head. 'Some poor fucker.' He turned his face into the cool morning breeze, and they made their way towards the gate and the long drive home.

* * *

Helen sat down as commanded, crossed her legs and waited. The man who had driven her from the caravan reappeared, dragging something heavy and metal.

Sol stared at her. 'I know why you came here, Helen.'

Helen turned to look behind her. 'I told you why I came.'

'You did. But I know what you really wanted.'

Helen returned his look. 'I came here to make a deal. You're a businessman. I thought you'd be interested in a trade.'

'Helen, you're an intelligent woman but you're too . . . conditioned? Is that the right word in English? I'm still learning.'

'Conditioned?'

'Yes. You're used to people just doing what you say. You had power in your organisation, so you spoke to me as if the same rules applied here. They do not, Helen.'

'Rules?'

'The rules where people either do as you say or they don't. I work with a different set of rules. I'm surprised you're here at all. A woman of your intelligence shouldn't be so naïve.'

'I told you my situation. I know you can help me, and I came here because I can help you too.'

Helen could see the chains now. They were rusty, the sort that might hold a boat against a quay. The man dropped them and stood beside her. Sol nodded at him.

'Do you think I care about *mutually* beneficial? You destroy my family, and then you come here with no leverage. I am insulted that you even think I might accept your terms. It's like you're calling me weak. I am not weak, Helen.'

'I didn't think you were.'

'I think *you* are. Maybe you don't understand your situation. You are wanted by your own police force, for quite serious matters as far as I understand. No one knows you are here. You have no vehicle, no place to go, and the only leverage you have is some information about a couple of rats from my family's past.'

'I know you place a high value on that information, otherwise you *will* appear weak.'

Sol Alcani struck her so hard she rolled off the chair.

'You need to understand your position, Helen. You have two options.'

'Fuck you!' Helen struggled back onto the chair. Sol walked around it and stood looking down at her. He grabbed hold of her wrist and squeezed until she cried out.

'Two options, Helen. You give me the information you have, all of it, right now, and I let you walk away from here.'

Helen's anger made her brave. She looked straight at him. 'You won't get anything this way.'

Sol ignored the comment. 'Option two. You decide not to give me the information at this point. I get my man here to ask you for it again, but *after* he's stripped you naked and beaten you until he's too tired to carry on. And *then* he might decide that you're quite an attractive woman . . . Maybe he gets tired and calls the others over, and they take their turns. And when they're finished, I will give you one last opportunity to tell me. You will tell me, be sure of that. *Then* I will let you walk, but the odds of hiding in broad daylight, naked and beaten? I wouldn't fancy your chances.'

Helen said nothing.

'You don't need to be rushing your answer, Helen. We can speak after I've had my breakfast.' Sol turned away and was quickly out of sight.

The blow came out of nowhere. The blackness gradually faded, and she put out a hand to steady herself, unsure if she was falling. Someone pushed her upright and she felt the chain land on her shoulder. They wrapped the heavy metal around her and pulled it tight. Helen screamed.

The man gave it a last tug.

And then he was gone.

Chapter 15

She hadn't been difficult to find. George knew vehicles are often the key. Ryker must have told his wife not to use a vehicle registered in her name, and not to hire a car. So, through a friend, Sarah had unearthed an old Ford Fiesta. This friend's husband turned over a few cars from home and displayed his stock on his social media site. All George had to do was check the registration numbers against the ANPR database. Forty minutes after he started searching, he had found it. George had always been lucky with finding people. When he was in uniform his team had joked that people — and trouble — found *him*. How right they were.

The last ANPR ping for the car was just an hour ago. It had them coming off the main road outside Langhorne and into the Alkham Valley. This was a winding road that followed the bottom of an ancient valley and linked the town with a small hamlet called Kearsney. George knew exactly where they would be going. There was a picturesque walking and play area on the site of an old abbey where the waters from the valley combined to flow into rapids. They had often visited the place on a sunny Sunday afternoon.

Ryker would have told her not to follow any routines, and to behave totally out of character. Luckily for George, Sarah didn't like following instructions.

It was a twenty-minute drive. George grabbed his car keys.

* * *

George soon found the Fiesta. It was tucked into the space furthest from the road in the small car park. George pulled up his collar and followed the river. He didn't have to go far.

Wearing her polka-dot wellies, Charley was wading in the fast-moving shallow water. Another girl was with her, someone George didn't recognise. They both held brightly coloured fishing nets. Sarah sat on a bench with her back to him. The girls were engrossed in their fishing.

George considered just walking over to them. Sarah would be furious. But seeing his daughter, being close enough to hear her beautiful, carefree giggle — it was too much for him. He began to move towards them.

Suddenly his wife stood up. A man was approaching, heading straight for her, and her face lit up with a smile. They kissed. It was an intimate kiss. George's stomach knotted, and he stopped. He stood stock still for a moment, and then spun on his heels and hurried away.

Back in the car park, George stopped at the Ford Fiesta and checked over his shoulder. He was a good distance from where he had seen his wife. She wouldn't be coming back anytime soon.

The Fiesta was a darkish red and nondescript, its paintwork rusting in places. George pulled a rectangular object, a little smaller than his smartphone, out of his jacket pocket. He rubbed at the magnetic base, and checked around him. No one was taking any notice of him. He dropped to his knees and switched on the device. He felt around behind the front bumper, looking for a flat steel plate. The magnet sucked at the steel with a satisfying *clunk*.

George walked out of the car park, crossed the road and followed the path for a few hundred metres, until he came to a pub. Parked outside was an unmarked Skoda Fabia. He slipped into the driver's seat and selected an app on his phone that showed a map. A red tag dropped onto the car park by the river. The GPS tracker was more accurate than he had hoped.

* * *

'Hey!' Emily looked up from her computer screen. The woman was wearing a CSI uniform, and Emily didn't recognise her. She looked around at the desks and then made to leave.

'Can I help you?' asked Emily.

The woman turned. 'I was hoping to speak to George Elms.'

'He's popped out of the office for a while.' Emily checked her watch. 'I reckon he should be back pretty soon.'

'Oh, okay, no worry. If you could tell him Ali popped in, and maybe he can give me a call?'

Emily's curiosity was piqued. It wasn't often they had a visit from one of the forensic team. 'The kettle's just boiled. I'm Emily Ryker, by the way. I'm working with George on this whole thing. I'm his personal intel officer really.' She smiled.

'Okay, I guess I could have a quick cuppa. I'm trying to stay out of the office at the moment. I should be heading back out by now.'

'Perfect!' Emily switched on the kettle.

Ali grinned. 'I thought you said it had just boiled?'

'And there's me thinking I was the detective.'

'You get an eye for detail in my job too.'

'I bet.' Emily sat down. 'Is that what brings you up here? Your eye for detail?'

Ali peered around the office. Emily guessed she was checking that they were alone. Ali bit her lip, and then seemed to come to a decision. 'We had a positive on the voluntary DNA samples after the chief was shot. I haven't compared it to any of the other scenes yet, but it matched with a hair fibre from the motorcycle helmet that was found.'

Emily sat forward. 'Go on.'

'One of the hotel workers. The worksheet that accompanied the sample has his name as Kane Mitchell. He was part of the front–of-house team.'

'Hotel staff?'

'Yeah, the Hythe Imperial. After the shooting we chose some busy locations and got voluntary swabs from people. Took hours. It was one of the longest days I think I've ever worked . . . Anyway, this guy worked at the Imperial.'

'That is interesting. So he did the shooting, rode his bike to Hythe, ditched it beside the canal then made it on foot to the hotel, where he blended back in with his colleagues. And he did this all with an injury?'

'This is the point where you really have to do some detective work. All I can say is that his sample matches with the motorcycle helmet worn by whoever was riding that bike.'

Emily shook her head. 'Someone shot the chief of police in the middle of the day, rode off, shot a second man dead in his own kitchen and then disappeared. It's almost beyond belief. Maybe we should start believing in the impossible!'

'Who knows what happened?'

'And you're only just getting results on this now?'

'We took thousands of samples. The hotel staff were deemed to be a very low priority, there was some debate as to whether they were sent off at all. It's very costly.'

'And isn't that what matters. We'll do everything we can to find the man shooting dead police officers, as long as it's cost effective.'

Ali shrugged, 'We get the same message all the time. I dread to think how many low-level burglaries could be resolved if we were actually sending off the DNA hits. If the victims only knew.'

Emily stood up. 'Tea or coffee?'

'Tea, please. I don't think I've had one all day.'

'No tea all day? I don't think I could work like that. I guess the house shooting has kept you lot busy today?' asked Emily, fishing.

Ali smiled. 'That's where I should be right now. You heard about it then?'

'I don't know anything more than that there was a shooting,' Emily lied.

Ali sighed. 'Ah well. Always a long day when you get a double murder.'

'A double murder?' Emily raised an eyebrow.

'A male and a female — husband and wife.'

'What was that about then?' Emily busied herself with the tea, feigning indifference.

'Who knows? There's very little at the scene to go on. From the look of the house, they just seemed like an ordinary couple. I guess you just never know, do you?' Ali shrugged.

'They must have pissed someone off though.'

'My colleague reckons it's a professional hit. You have to really piss off the wrong person to earn that fate. We don't see many of them down here.'

'Professional? What makes them think that?' This was something Emily didn't know.

'You learn to tell these things. The scene was too clean for a start, just the two dead bodies and a single splatter, know what I mean?'

'I'm not sure I do. That doesn't sound very clean to me.' Emily was bluffing again.

Ali counted on her fingers. 'No sign of any disturbance, no forced entry, everywhere left locked, no other wounds on the victims, nothing stolen. They definitely weren't killed in a fight or tortured for the code to their safe. They didn't stand a chance. They probably never even saw it coming.'

'Scary shit.' Emily held out a cup.

'Thanks. Yeah. We've seen something like it before. My colleague happened to attend a similar job. Reckons it was easily seven years ago but the same MO.'

Emily raised her eyebrows over the rim of her cup. 'We know the MO then?'

'Not for sure. You never really do with a professional hit. But Terry said that last one was just the same. Body in the hallway, no sign of a break-in, shot in the head at close range and still wearing their outdoor clothes. They reckon the shooter cut the power, see, so whoever came in was a sitting duck. Seven years ago the entry wound was upwards into the neck, and it was the same today.'

Emily put her cup down. 'So he hides on the floor in the dark and, what? Waits for the poor fucker to trip over him? How would you know he turned the electrics off? Guesswork?'

'Well, Terry said that they never found a print, a strand of hair, nothing. After going over the place for several days all they found was a smudge.'

'A smudge?' Emily echoed.

'Yeah. In the cupboard under the stairs. There was a smudge on the dust of the main fuse switch. The bullet was fired upwards through the victim's neck, so the theory was that he turned the power off, then hid in the cupboard. The first thing you do when you flick a switch and nothing happens is go to the fuse box in the cupboard, isn't it?'

'And what? There was a smudge today?'

Ali nodded. 'There was. We couldn't be sure but a UV photo shows recent disturbance. Not a print — our killer was careful. Just a smudge.'

'Another smudge.' Emily began to feel like a chorus.

'Exactly. The male was shot from the floor too. The bullet entered his front teeth and it was moving upward. It went out through the top of his head. Maybe it's just a coincidence . . .' Ali shrugged.

'Maybe. Us detectives don't believe in coincidences though, Ali.'

'CSIs are the same.'

George Elms swept in past Ali and threw his bag onto his desk.

'Alright?' Emily called out.

'Yeah. Dandy,' George replied, and nodded at Ali.

'Kettle's just boiled.' Emily raised her cup.

'Great.'

Emily indicated the CSI. 'Ali's come to tell us there's been a hit on the DNA from the motorcycle helmet.'

'Ah, the helmet. Yes, I read about that. Wasn't it found close to the second murder scene after the chief was shot?' George had actually read the report closely.

Emily nodded. 'Thassit. Hit on Kane Mitchell.'

George thumped the table. 'Mitchell! That's the name he gave.'

'He was working at the Hythe Imperial, front of house. We need to get down there, George, see what people know about him. Who knows, he might even still be there. He might even park our car for us.' Emily giggled.

George didn't even break a smile. 'It's a waste of time, Ryker.' He stood looking at his computer screen.

'How is it a waste? It's the last place we know he was!'

'We're not going to find him by going to places he *was,* Ryker. Don't you get it? The DNA was a *voluntary* thing, right? That means that he gave his sample knowing we would match it up. He knows we will go down to the hotel and trace his movements. He *knows* that, Ryker, because he knows what we're going to do before we do ourselves. It's all part of his fucking game. He controls our movements by leaving breadcrumbs for us to sniffle at, like little squirrels.'

'I've got to get back to it.' Ali put her half-empty cup on the desk and strode out of the room.

Emily took a breath and managed to swallow her retort. 'So what do *you* want to do?'

George put down his mouse and spun to face her. 'He's a criminal, and he's getting resources from somewhere. He's being hidden, he's firing guns, and he's shooting people at the top end of the drug supply chain. All that means that there are other criminals who know something about him. That's your remit, Ryker. Get me some intel I can use. I'm two years out of the loop. Get me a list of the main drug suppliers, and the people who sell guns. I want to know who's shifting the most gear on the streets. At least one of them knows something about Kane fucking Forley or Mitchell, or whatever he's going by. Get me something that can help us find him.'

Emily folded her arms. 'You're not angry at me, George.'

'Maybe I am. Maybe I'm angry at anyone who isn't helping me right now. Get me that intel by the end of the day. Then I can get out there and find out what these people know. Send a fucking chimp out to the hotel and have him write down the three-month-old intel, 'cause I ain't wasting my time with it.' He turned away.

Emily spoke to his back. 'Of course you know better, George. You just try holding out that badge and asking the dealers what they know. You're gonna get nothing but a stony silence. I've seen it a million times, so don't talk to me like it's my fucking first day. Criminals don't tell police about other criminals unless they have to, and we haven't got anything to offer, have we?'

'Bullshit.'

'Think about it. How many times have you flashed your badge at someone and got a straight answer? It doesn't work. It never has.' Emily shook her head.

'I want a list of people by the end of the day. Maybe I have no intention of just asking. Ed Kavski was scum, but he taught us a thing or two about getting information on criminals.'

'And how did Ed Kavski end up, George? Think about that!'

Emily didn't watch him storm out of the office. She'd already turned away.

Chapter 16

Emily was still angry when she entered the public library. It had once been a church, and the hushed atmosphere went well with its new role. They sold good coffee too. Emily took her mug to one of the computers and waited to be authorised by the library assistant, who seemed to be struggling.

Her terminal became active at last and Emily gave the woman at the counter a thumbs-up. The email account already showed a new message in drafts. Emily glanced around. She was pretty much on her own.

It took a few moments for the message to appear.

There's something going on, the family are busy, they're on the fucking warpath. Took someone out last night, some other poor fucker chained to a chair this morning. All is not rosy. We need to talk about my exit.

Emily sniffed. It was not going to be easy to arrange an exit for him. He'd been on a crew a few years now. He was even running one, and from what she could determine, he was getting jobs done. They didn't let people like that just walk away, not without asking a lot of questions. She highlighted the body of the email, and it disappeared when she typed her reply.

It's all possible. The one way we mess up an exit is by rushing it. You will get an opportunity to go, usually it just happens with time but we can manufacture a way out. We just need to think things through, wait for the right moment.

Emily saved the draft and sipped at her coffee. She logged out of the email account and into Facebook. She only used it to track criminals but when there really was nothing else to do she liked to peer in on other peoples' lives. She saw that it was fifteen years to the day since she had left school. One of her friends was now a housewife with a rich husband, the sort that 'did lunch' every day and complained about everything. Emily was becoming increasingly jealous of people outside the police. Imagine worrying about what time to get up to get to the *Next* sale, or where to get the dog manicured! 'Heaven is a place where nothing ever happens,' she said aloud. 'Ain't that the truth!'

It had been long enough. Emily logged back into her email and clicked on the new draft.

We need to get 'manufacturing.' I need to be getting out. I've got a bad feeling about all this. Can we meet?

'Fuck!' said Emily, and looked around to make sure no one had heard. She'd never run an undercover before. She hadn't ever wanted to. She really couldn't cope with getting a copper killed. The golden rule was to avoid having the UC agent contact any known officers. Ever. Emily was a known officer.

We don't need to meet, it makes you vulnerable. We can sort this without. I saw the overnight report from here, your job was well timed, the shooting has taken the focus off it. Lennockshire have got no idea and I don't think there will be too much focus either.

I know it's a tense time over there. You keep doing what you're doing and this could work well for us. The family won't be letting anyone else in, they'll move people up from within, this could be when you really get in among it.

Emily hoped she sounded encouraging. Trying to talk this man into staying put made her feel guilty. It was easy for her. Here she was, drinking her coffee, a safe distance between her and the foremost crime family in the county. She quickly logged back into the account, knowing she would have a reply. It wasn't what she hoped for.

We need to meet. I will call you when I can. If you don't answer I will walk into the station and become your problem.

'Fuck!' Emily swore again, and typed rapidly.

Don't be silly. I'm just saying that we need to be careful. For your sake.

Tell me a time. We'll talk.

Emily closed the email account. She was about to shut down the terminal but clicked back into Facebook. Another ex-school friend had posted a picture of her new set of nails. They were pretty too, each one slightly different. 'Fuck that,' Emily said, and picked up her coffee.

Chapter 17

George walked back into the office. There was no one there. He'd wasted twenty minutes and a pound on a shit coffee from the top floor. He should have bitten his tongue and stayed where he was.

A piece of paper sat on top of his keyboard. He recognised Emily's handwriting. It gave a list of names with one-word offences next to them, and a reference number so he could find them on his computer. She had signed off with a cartoon picture of a penis. He noticed that his screen was now on and waiting for his password. He felt bad. He knew he wasn't angry at her. It wasn't Emily's fault. But fuck it, it had gotten him some of the information he needed.

He scanned the list. Six names. Two were people supplying the area with class A, both from Merseyside. One was thought to be the main man running the dealing on the frontline, then a couple of active burglars. The last one caught his eye.

'Carl Matten,' he said aloud. Emily had written a brief summary next to his name: *Also part of the Scouse line. They've got a foothold in Langthorne since Kavski. Matten's fallen out with the line, he's got desperate and turned to robbing other dealers — intel states he's using a firearm. Most recent intel is that he's working with a London gang from Woolwich who have Ashford and want Langthorne. Source says he got the firearm local.*

George addressed the empty office. 'A firearm.' He clicked through a couple of screens on his computer, brought up *Matten* from a list of possibles, and readied a pen. He was showing NFA, but there were two addresses where he might be staying. Grabbing Emily's note, George scooped up the keys to the Skoda.

* * *

'Jesus, Mother and Mary.' It was a woman's voice. Helen must have fallen asleep. Even the smallest movement caused her pain, and the effort of keeping herself still for so long had worn her out. Her whole body hurt. She lifted her head, and winced.

'This is no way to be treating people,' the woman said. She stooped to look at Helen. From her dark brown eyes, Helen guessed she was an Alcani. The mother, maybe. The woman was smiling. It seemed genuine, caring even. She wore a vest top, and the skin of her arms was wrinkled.

'Do you have any water?' Helen rasped. She was parched. She was hungry too, but most of all she yearned to move her limbs and shake off the numbness.

'Jack-Jack!' The woman shouted across Helen. 'Jack-Jack! I don't care what he said, get over here and sort this out. This isn't how we treat our guests.' The woman had her hands on her hips.

Helen looked up at her. She heard a scuffling behind her, someone who dragged his feet. Just like the man who had trussed her up.

'Get her out of these.' The woman gestured at the chains.

'The boss, he said she stays here until he tells me different.'

'Who's the boss here, Jack-Jack? You already pissed me off. Don't be telling me no again.'

The man didn't reply. The woman didn't budge. Helen got the impression she was used to getting her way. Sure enough, the chains on her shoulder moved. It felt as if the blood pumping through her veins was suddenly boiling. The pain was excruciating.

'Thank you.' Helen closed her eyes.

'We women have got to look after each other around here.' She raised her voice. 'This isn't how we treat people.' His rough hands tugged the last chain clear of Helen's body.

'Can you stand?' asked the woman.

Helen rocked forward onto her legs. They took her weight.

'Good,' the woman said. 'Let's get you something to eat and drink.'

Helen limped after her to a truck parked just behind the 4x4, and managed somehow to haul herself up into the passenger seat.

'Who are you?' she said.

The woman smiled, and started the engine. 'Despite what the men out there seem to think, I'm the boss.'

* * *

The first address was empty. The second one looked more promising. Along the front was a row of shops — a convenience store, a Polish food shop, a launderette, a café and a kebab and pizza takeaway. The door to the flats above was at the rear. George concentrated on the kebab shop, since his target flat was directly above it. He could see a metal staircase leading up in that direction. There were two flats, one at each end of the landing. George could see part of the door to his target flat. It appeared to be made of pine, and opened inward, with a single lock halfway down. Perfect for rapid entry.

But George wasn't here for rapid entry. He wasn't actually sure what he was here for, but that didn't stop him jumping the wall into the rear yard and pacing silently towards the steps. He took them two at a time, up to the flat. There was a window on the next floor up, but none on his level. George had been in many similar places. The front door would most likely open into a hallway, with the main living rooms all at the far end, overlooking the street. The bathroom, and maybe a storage area, would be at the back. This meant that anyone inside the flat would be a long way from the door.

George considered his options. Quietly breaking into the flat of a suspected drug dealer, who might be sitting inside with a firearm and acute paranoia was not the best idea. But Emily's words rattled around in his mind. She was right. He'd get nothing by flashing his badge. They would have to be a lot less predictable if they wanted to find someone like Kane Forley.

George pulled a stiff piece of card from his inside pocket and worked at the lock. The door opened, and he heard noises inside, made by a man and a woman. The noises sounded like sex.

George had been pretty close with the layout. He made his way down a long corridor. The threadbare carpet was just enough to mask his footfalls, though he could have marched along in pit boots — the two occupants' attention was elsewhere.

The bedroom was off to the right at the end of the corridor. Light was coming from a room to the left and the door was ajar. George peered inside and caught sight of a woman's foot, moving in time to the thrusting of an older man with jeans and underwear around his ankles. George reckoned he was witnessing a business transaction, but whatever it was, it didn't involve Carl Matten.

George padded into the bedroom opposite. The room was sparsely furnished, its only features a canvas-sided wardrobe with two empty hangers, and a bed. George stepped further in, and noticed a sports hold-all stuffed with clothing. A T-shirt spilled out of the top, and a tracksuit lay next to it — men's clothing. George listened. The business transaction was clearly still in progress. He went over to the bag and held it upside down. It was heavier than it should be. A black handgun fell with a thud onto the carpet, and George stiffened. The noises from the other room continued.

George rifled through the bag, knowing that he might be pushing his luck. It contained clothes, and an Oyster card. George typed the reference number into his phone, to be used for tracing the owner if needed. He found two train tickets in the side pocket, both dated recently, one to London St Pancras and one for Liverpool Lime Street Station. George picked up the weapon. It fitted snugly in his grip. The noises next door reached a crescendo. George needed to leave. He looked at the weapon in his hand and made a decision. He checked the safety and stuffed it into his waistband.

George left the property the same way he came in, only this time he slammed the door, enjoying the thought of the panicked dismount. He'd left the contents of the bag tipped out, so the occupant could tell Matten they'd been burgled. Maybe that way she wouldn't get the blame for stealing his weapon.

He made it back to the boundary wall and returned to the Skoda, yawning. He wasn't used to working and he was dead tired and hungry. The smell of pizza wafted up his nostrils and he thought of Emily. Maybe she hadn't eaten yet, and turning up with hot food might just serve as an apology.

He hated saying sorry.

Chapter 18

'You're the copper?'

'Ex.' Helen accepted a second glass of water and drank it more slowly.

'I hear they're looking for you.'

'Yes.'

'Why?'

'I got involved with a criminal. They don't like that.'

The woman smiled. 'So you didn't learn your lesson?'

'It would appear not.'

'I grew up with strict parents, who tried to teach me right from wrong. Then I met Nial, and married into all this.' The woman swept an arm around the vast farmhouse kitchen. Helen had seen the inside of the house before, but only in pictures taken on the day of the raid. It was the only original building left on the Alcani site. 'And you know what, I'm not so sure about right and wrong anymore. Know what I mean?'

Helen nodded. 'I think I do.'

'I mean, you police have all the power. They came here — twenty of them there was — bashed the door in, searched the house from top to bottom. They took all our mobile phones, laptops, my iPad, the lot. I still haven't got most of it back. If *I* did that, you'd call it burglary.'

Helen found that she could still laugh. 'I've never thought of it like that.'

'Well, you don't, do you? You get brainwashed, not by right and wrong, but by your power. And then you stop caring about what actually is right and wrong, just about what you can put people in prison for. I see it all the time. You're looking for the bad in people so much that you can't see any of the good.'

Helen sighed. She was too exhausted to argue. 'What's your name?' she asked.

'You mean you don't know?' I thought I was famous where you come from.'

'I hear a lot of names,' Helen said.

'Rosalina. I get called Rosie.'

'Well, Rosie, thank you. That is a name I know. That makes Sol your son, right? Won't he be angry with you?'

'He should be more worried about me being angry with him. We're better than what you went through today, really. But since your people took his father away, he's just angry.'

'I came here to offer him some answers. So he could channel that anger towards the right people.'

Rosie got up and pulled open the oven door. 'Should be about done. You must be starving.'

'Yeah, I didn't get the chance to eat much today.' The women shared a wry smile.

'He's not a bad boy. Typical man is all. They only have one way of doing anything, and that's heavy-handed. He wants information, he asks the only way he knows how. He doesn't think about who he's asking. Some people will talk to you, but you have to treat them with respect. Some people deserve a little explanation.'

Rosie dropped a large helping of cheesy pasta into a bowl and pushed it towards Helen. She began to slice a loaf of bread.

'So you have different ways of doing things, Rosie. Is this what this is?'

Rosie stood with the knife poised. 'You are going to have to tell them boys what you know. I can make sure they look after you when you do, but I can't keep them away if you don't.'

'Well, thank you, Rosie, for your support. But as soon as I give up all I have, your boys won't need me anymore. I've had a little taste of how that might end.'

'Then tell me.' Rosie's gaze became intense. 'Talk to me about what you know, and let me deal with the boys. They'll listen to me.'

'So this is your way of asking differently? Helen indicated the meal.

'You are going to have to tell them boys out there,' Rosie repeated. 'Lord help you if you don't.'

'Lord help me if I do.'

Rosie bit her bottom lip. Very deliberately, she laid the knife on the table.

Helen picked up her fork. 'This looks delicious.'

Rosie reached forward and pulled back the bowl.

'It's no good, Sol.' Her voice was suddenly louder. She was still facing Helen, and staring intently at her.

Helen's eyes widened. Sol Alcani appeared from behind his mother.

He chuckled. 'I told you, ma. I said she was too stubborn.'

'Too stupid more like.' Rosie's expression had lost its warmth.

Helen stood up, looking for something she could use. But there was nothing within reach.

'I gave you a chance, you stupid bitch!' Rosie was shaking her head.

Someone grabbed Helen by her hair, pulling her head backwards. She tried to scratch at his hand to free herself. The man swore and pulled harder. Some of her hair came away in his grasp. He yanked her backwards towards the door.

Helen tried not to scream as he dragged her towards the warehouse.

Chapter 19

'We need to talk.'

She gasped. It was her flat, she lived alone and no one had keys. But that voice was only too familiar. Jana swung her shopping bags onto the kitchen table and switched on the light. Kane Forley sat with his hands steepled, speaking from his seat under the window. An empty cup rested by his feet.

'My phone, it is dead.' Jana held it out.

'A bit of simple pre-planning.'

'I'm sorry, I didn't know.'

'What can you tell me?'

Jana shrugged and held her palms out. 'Nothing more. I tell you when I see you yesterday.'

'Nothing more?'

'Nothing more. It's normal, nothing.'

Kane stamped on the floor and Jana jumped again.

'The accent, Jana. It can really grate sometimes, especially when you're whining. Now, I gave you a specific task.'

'I told you I am not able to do what you ask all the time. I clean. I go places where I clean and sometimes there is no one.'

'It doesn't take a massive amount of imagination to get to places where there *are* people, does it? You don't even need to be in the same room. The police write everything down. They have to, for fuck's sake.'

'I told you information. I tell you everything. I tell you the old man looking for you, and you kill him. I tell you Mr Lance is in charge and I put phone on his roof. I tell you George is back but he only works with the woman.'

'You need to be useful, Jana. You remember what happens when you're not useful?

'I tell you everything.'

'I told you, I want to know what they know. The whole thing rests on you, Jana.' Kane got to his feet and moved close to her. Jana stepped back until she was pressed against the kitchen work surface. Kane ran the back of his index finger across her face and between her lips. She recoiled, and he smiled.

'I'm going to ask you to do something different for me. Seeing as how you've found it so difficult, I'll ask for something easier.'

'You said I needed to find out the names of the people. Who was looking for you again. I did. This was the deal, no?'

'No!' Kane suddenly grabbed her by the neck and forced her head backwards. He held her for a few seconds, then suddenly let go and stepped back. He sat down again.

'I need some very specific information, Jana. Does that sound easy enough for you?'

'I can't, I can't always get. If I get caught, I—'

'What!' Kane leapt up and kicked her in the ribs. It knocked her off her feet. He stood looking down at her.

'You will do what I ask or I will go and get your fourteen-year-old bitch sister and I will give her back to those men who were selling her on the street for a tenner a go. Do you understand me?'

Jana curled into a ball and sobbed into the carpet. Kane bent down and put his mouth close to her ear. 'Do you?'

Jana jerked her head. He stepped over her and opened the front door.

'I will be back soon, Jana, and you need to have done better. You told me you would help, remember? Remember how you felt when the police did nothing to help you or your family? How angry you were? You and me, we're going to make them pay, Jana. Wait for my instructions. Don't fuck this up now!'

He slammed the front door behind him.

It was some time before she dared look up.

Chapter 20

The evening was noticeably cooler and Emily had put on a warm jumper. It was more than up to the job of keeping her outside on the patio listening to the sea shuffle the pebbles around on the beach below. No gin tonight. Instead she settled for a cup of tea. That morning she had woken up tired, with a slightly muzzy head. It was only eight o'clock and she was already fighting off a yawn.

She noticed a figure on the promenade. All the walls had been built low to give a sea view, but this meant that people often walked across the bottom of her garden. On a sunny day there could be hundreds of them. It never really bothered Emily. She didn't like sunbathing and only really used the patio in the evening. This figure, however, walked past and then came back and stopped at her wall. She couldn't be sure if it was looking directly at her or not. Then it stepped over her wall and made its way up to her patio.

Emily snatched up her phone, but the figure was on her before she could even unlock it.

'You won't need that, Ryker!' George chuckled.

'Fuck!' Emily exclaimed. 'I thought it was some weirdo.' She paused. 'Turns out I was right.'

'Very good.' George sat down and placed a carrier bag on the table. It smelt like hot food.

'Please have a seat,' Emily quipped. 'What's that?'

'Chinese food. I didn't want to eat on my own tonight, so that means you eat with me or you watch me eat.'

'I had my induction at the gym tonight.'

'Oh.' George had a plastic tub in his hand. 'Does that mean you're on some kind of diet or something?'

'Does it fuck! It means I can justify it.'

George grinned and went back to pulling the tops off tubs and laying them out on the table.

Emily got to her feet. 'I'll get some cutlery then.' She reappeared almost immediately. 'Hang on. I never told you my address!'

George snatched a spoon from her hand. 'I'm a detective, Ryker.'

'You mean you abused your power as a supervisor and looked at the personnel records?'

'I didn't, actually. They have only given me limited access. I got another skipper to do it.' George crunched a prawn cracker.

'You wanna be careful, George. You could get in a lot of trouble.'

'I wouldn't worry. Lennockshire Police are pretty lax. They let anyone off.'

'So this is your apology then, is it? It's actually not a bad one.'

'I guess so. Though it did kill two birds with one stone. I really didn't fancy eating on my own again.'

'Are you feeling lonely, George Elms?'

George shrugged.

'Did you get what you wanted from the intel I left?'

George nodded. 'Yeah, that was the sort of stuff. I just feel like we're not getting anywhere near this bloke, you know? I know I can do it, but it will take a bit of time. Trouble is, we don't have time.'

Emily looked at him. 'You're convinced he's got something planned for us, aren't you?'

'Why wouldn't he? And he's going to want to top what he's already put us through. I was lying awake last night, thinking about the whole thing. He's never been more dangerous.'

'How so?' Emily put down her spoon.

'We know who he is, and he knows that we do. He knew it the second I got released.'

'How does that make him more dangerous? Surely, now he has to run?'

'I don't think so. If he does, he risks getting caught — by me. He couldn't accept that. I think he's coming straight at us. Shit or bust.'

Emily shook her head. 'I don't fancy either of those options.'

'He gave the police a trail to follow, knowing it would end with me getting out.'

'So, what? He has some sort of grand plan, and you're part of it?'

'I think so, yeah. He certainly knows how to carry through a plan.'

'Maybe it's some sort of blaze of glory thing. Like Billy the Kid.'

George nodded. 'That would fit.'

'The press release goes out tonight,' said Emily. 'He'll be everywhere by the morning. I got his mug shot from the driving license people. He looks like a psycho.'

George paused, his laden fork in the air. 'I said it was a mistake, but Lewis wouldn't listen to me. We should play for time. Kane likes to wait to be provoked, so he has someone to blame.'

'So what now? I guess you've given up rattling the people lower down?'

'I've not given it up completely. Tonight just showed that it needs time.'

Emily raised her eyebrows. 'Tonight? What happened tonight?'

'I went looking for one of your tip-offs, Carl Matten. I fancy he's my way in.'

Emily finished her mouthful. 'What the fuck did you do that for? What do you mean you went looking for him?'

The sudden anger in her voice seemed to catch George off guard. 'Just that. I went looking for him. You said he's got recent form for robbing drug dealers with a gun. So where did he get it from? It might just be the same bloke that is supplying our man. Or at least I can find out who the competition is.'

'Jesus, George! That intel was clearly marked *sensitive*. Matten has only been in the area a couple of weeks, and that was source information. The source is close to him, sharing his bed in fact, and she's the only one that could know. You go storming in there demanding to know where he gets his guns from and you will get *her* killed.'

'I know how to handle sensitive information, Ryker.'

'Well, clearly you don't.'

'I didn't think—'

'That's right,' Emily cut in. She hit the table with her fork. 'You don't think, do you? You just storm in there like nothing else matters. These people might be shits, George, they might not matter to you, but when they come to me I have to promise to keep them safe, and I look into their eyes when I say it!'

'Okay, Emily, okay. I didn't find him. Someone else was there, and they had no idea.'

'What do you mean they had no idea? You peeked through their window?'

'No, I slipped in the door. I was very quiet. I saw who was in there and it wasn't Matten, so I left. No harm done.'

'No harm done? That sums you up, that does. No harm done! Carl Matten wouldn't think twice about putting a gun to my source's head if he had an inkling she was talking to me. What if you'd found him there? What were you planning to do then?'

'I don't know, Emily. I didn't really think it through. I know it was stupid—'

'Too fucking right it was stupid, George. I'm telling you now, this isn't working. Not for me, not for us. You think you can do what you like as far as I'm concerned and I'll just tag along. Well, I won't. You should go.'

'Ryker — Emily — don't be silly.'

'Don't call me silly, George. Don't talk to me like I'm some fucking newbie! If I fuck up, these people die. Well, I clearly fucked up giving you this intel in the first place. And you know what? I only did it because it's you. Because you have this sort of spell over me, and it makes me angry. I mean, what was I doing?' Emily's voice had risen.

'Emily, look, no harm done. I fucked up, not you.'

'This can't work George. Me and you, I mean. With you like *this*. This work is important. I'm going back up north. I'll sort it out tomorrow and then I'll be gone. Things won't end well if I stay here. I can just see that something bad is going to happen around you.'

'You mean like happened to everyone else?' George's voice took on an edge.

'No. That isn't what I meant. Just that you're on some sort of rampage. Look, I get it. This is real personal for you. I understand, but I can't support you. I won't be here tomorrow, I'm sorry. I'll speak to the bosses, tell them that I want to go back up to the north of the county. I'm already way over my time down here, it's always been made clear that I can go back at any time.' Emily got to her feet and carried her plate over to the patio door.

George remained seated.

'Finish your food, yeah.' Emily glanced at his half-full plate. 'I'll see you around, maybe.'

Chapter 21

At seven the next morning, George Elms sat at a desk tucked away in an alcove opposite his office. It was used for reviewing sensitive information. He knew Emily well enough to know that she meant what she said. She wouldn't be back. He would need to be his own source of local knowledge from now on. He used her list as his starting point.

A cup of tea — his second — steamed away under the screen.

He heard a thud, followed by the sound of a mug bouncing on a carpeted floor. It seemed to come from his incident room. George checked his watch. It was early for anyone to be in.

He got to his feet and paced into the incident room, expecting to see Paul Baern. It wasn't. Instead of a balding, middle-aged man with a lopsided smile he found a slim, twenty-something woman, bending to pick up a blue notebook.

'You okay?' The girl jumped like George had dug a stick in her ribs. She winced and put her hand to her side, as if he had done just that.

'Sorry,' she spluttered. 'I knocked off, cleaning.'

George recognised Jana, the regular cleaner. 'It's okay. Here, let me help.' He bent and picked up the mug, which had rolled under a desk. Then his eye went to the notebook. Jana still held it, pressed tight to her chest.

'Did you need that?' George gestured towards it. Jana started, and almost dropped it again. She put it on the desktop.

'I try not to move too many things. They say I should wipe the desks down. I don't get chance in here, the door locks.'

'It does. I'm in early today. It's fine, it's nice to have it clean. If there's no one in here, though, don't worry about cleaning. Okay?'

Jana nodded. 'Okay, sure. Would you just like me to leave a cloth? Some polish maybe? Other rooms with locks, they ask me to just leave some cleaning and I replace it. Just leave the bins outside the door and I change for you.'

George smiled at her. 'Sure, good idea. I'm sure we can manage to wipe our own desks.' Jana smiled back, seeming less nervous now.

'Are you in pain? What happened?' George gestured at her hand, still held to her side.

'Yes, I sleep bad.'

'You hurt yourself in *bed*?' He stared at her.

'Yes, I wake up and sore. I don't explain so well, sometimes my back, sometimes the side.'

George shrugged. 'Maybe you need to get yourself a new bed, one that treats you better.'

She smiled again. 'Maybe.'

George looked at the name stitched on her chest. 'Jana. Did I pronounce that right?'

'Jana, yes.'

'You take care of yourself, Jana, okay?'

She backed away, turned quickly and left.

George was still standing in the middle of the room when Paul Baern came in. He had seen Jana leave.

Paul grinned. 'Still the old charmer I see.'

'She was in here.'

'Yes, she was,' Paul replied.

'See what you can find out about her, Paul. I'm going to see where she goes.' He moved towards the door.

'I imagine she goes to the next part of the building that needs cleaning,' Paul offered. 'Look, is there any chance you can bring me up to speed? I can be a lot more useful if I know what the fuck is going on.'

'Just let me make a call, Paul. I want to find out what time she clocks off. The cleaners here, you only ever see them early in the morning, right? She could be off soon.'

Paul shrugged, took his bag off his shoulder and put it on the nearest seat. He indicated the desk in front of it. 'Anywhere, I presume.'

But George already had his phone to his ear. He nodded at his mate and switched on the kettle.

Chapter 22

George spotted the signs. Jana strode away from the police station, looking back too often over her shoulder. She was either surveillance aware, or paranoid. George was hoping it was the latter. He was observing from a ground-floor window. He wanted to see which way she turned before he made his move. The street was wide and empty and he would be visible if he emerged too soon.

Jana continued straight on, and then got into a taxi which was facing east. It pulled away just as George came out of the police station.

'Dammit!' The taxi was maybe 100 metres away and disappearing from view. He was confident he recognised the make and model and he could just make out the *Langthorne Taxis* sign at its back window. That should be enough to track it down.

George felt in his pocket and took out a key. The small Skoda seemed to have become his for keeps. The taxi office was a five-minute drive away. He checked his phone and found a missed call from Paul Baern. He switched on the ignition and called him back.

'George! Where are you? What's going on?'

'I'm in the car park with the engine running. I'll see you in a sec.' George hung up. There would be plenty of time for getting Paul up to speed. Right now he was more intent on finding out something he knew nothing about.

* * *

They drove to the taxi rank in silence. Paul was pissed off. He had expected to come back to a slick team of detectives, chasing down the man that had given them so much pain. Instead, here he was with a man still harbouring trust issues and who was not giving up any information. And where were the rest of the *team?*

'Where's Emily?' he asked eventually.

'She quit. She doesn't want to be part of this thing, and since I haven't got time for anyone who feels like that, it's worked out well.'

Paul left it there. He was being left in the dark. Fine. But he wouldn't put up with it for long. George pulled up at a taxi rank.

Paul didn't bother to unbuckle his seat belt. 'I suppose you don't even want me to come in.'

George got out. After a few seconds he ducked back in.

'I found that cleaner in our office this morning. It seemed odd to me. I just want to make sure she's not our leak.'

'She's a cleaner. She goes into every room. There must be more, surely?'

'No. Not really. It just didn't feel right. I'm sorry, but I'm extra sensitive right now, Paul. You might have to let me strike a few misses.'

Paul shrugged. 'Does she work here too?'

'No. I saw her get into one of their taxis when she left the nick. I want to know where they took her. If I can get her home address it'll be a start.'

'The start of what? A stalking episode?'

‘She was holding Ryker’s daybook. And the way she reacted to me, you know, it just wasn’t right.’

‘Alright, I get it.’ Paul opened his door. He had to wait for the traffic before he could get out. By then, George was in the taxi office, holding up his badge and berating the staff.

‘Of course you can tell me! It’s important. I’m leading an investigation here and I need to know where that driver was heading.’ George sounded frustrated and impatient. A sure-fire way to get people’s backs up.

‘And you didn’t get the registration number?’ The lad behind the Perspex screen looked annoyed.

‘No. It was a black Volkswagen Passat estate and it looked new. There can’t be many of them on your books.’

‘We don’t have *books*. All the drivers are self-employed. They drive their own cars.’

‘Well, thanks for the economics lesson. Is there an adult here I can speak to at all?’

Paul could see that the lad was about to clam up. He put a hand on George’s shoulder and muttered, ‘Give me a sec.’

Paul smiled at the lad. ‘Hi, mate. What’s your name?’

‘Liam.’

‘Thanks, Liam. I’m Paul. This is Detective Sergeant George Elms and we need your help to trace a journey. How many drivers have you got on today?’

‘He don’t need to speak to me like that. Just ’cause he’s a sergeant or whatever.’

‘You’re right. We’re all a bit stressed out at the moment. Sometimes we really need some information but we can’t tell people why, you know? We can’t tell them that it’s a matter of life or death, for example, even if we really want to. Do you get what I mean? Some of our greatest heroes have been normal civvies who never even knew what they did.’

The lad leaned forward in his seat and his eyes lit up. ‘Is this like a kidnapping or something?’

'Definitely not. And your driver isn't in any trouble. But we need to know where he went.'

'Alright, I'll give him a call.'

'Just give me his number and I'll call him.' George put out his hand.

Paul pushed the hand aside. 'I'll speak to him.'

'Your sergeant don't have to be like that, not with me. I ain't done nothing wrong.' He wrote down a mobile number, and handed it to Paul.

'Thanks for your help, Liam.'

* * *

'Why were you giving the kid a hard time in there?' Paul switched off the car radio.

'He was pissing about.'

'He was doing his job. He nearly told us to fuck off, and if I had been in that seat I would have told us to fuck off too.'

'You mean me.'

'Yeah, I mean you. He ain't the bloke we're pissed at.'

'Paul, I keep trying to make people understand that we don't get close to this bloke by being nice. We can't work how we usually do. We need results and we need them instantly. If people are getting in the way, we need to do a bit of bulldozing.'

'If he had wanted to, that lad in there could have made us fill out some ball-aching data protection form. Then forced us to wait a couple of days while it was signed off by somebody higher.'

'He was never going to do that. The lad was out of his depth the second we walked in there.' George pulled the Skoda out into the stream of traffic.

'Don't be treating people like that when I'm with you, or I will be rethinking my decision to come back. You appear to have alienated yourself from the rest of your team, so I reckon you need me. Whether you like it or not.'

'I'll drop you back, Paul. And I don't need anyone.'

* * *

When they stopped at Langthorne House, George didn't watch Paul walk away. He had his mobile phone in his hand, already punching in the numbers from the post-it note that Paul had slapped onto the dashboard. The phone rang once. It sounded like someone using hands-free and moving.

'Colin, Langthorne Taxis.'

'Colin, I got your number from your office. Do you have a fare on board?'

There was a pause. 'Not at the moment. I don't normally take direct calls. Where do you want me to come to?'

'Langthorne police station.'

'Okay. And where can I take you?'

'It's nothing like that, Colin. I just need to speak to you. I need a few details on your last fare. I'm a detective sergeant based here.'

Another pause. 'Well, okay, but I've just dropped in Dover so I've got maybe fifteen, twenty minutes back.'

'Dover? Don't worry, I'll come to you. Whereabouts in Dover are you?'

'Western Heights, by the castle.'

'Perfect. Pull into the coach park opposite the castle and I'll be there as soon as.'

'Well, okay, but time is money for us cabbies.'

'I'll make it worth your while, don't worry.'

* * *

Colin was waiting, the only car in the place. He stood beside it, an e-cigarette billowing out a cloud of smoke. He was small, with hair like an ageing rocker and boots to match.

'Take it you're the police sergeant?'

George entered the vaped cloud. 'Cherry?' he asked.

'Could be. They do all sorts of flavours. I never know what one's what.'

'Good as the real thing?'

'Not even close, but the wife, you know, she's keen for me to give it a go.'

George nodded. 'This won't take long. I'm interested in the girl you took home from the police station.'

Colin looked confused. 'Interested?'

'Yeah, as part of a criminal investigation. Don't get me wrong, she's not the criminal. I just want to be sure we can protect her if we need to.'

'I know what you mean. I get them all the time in 'ere.' He gestured with his thumb. 'The way a lot of these blokes talk to their girls, threats and that, you know? You wouldn't do it in my day. My wife would knock my block off!'

'It's a lot more common than people think.'

'Pretty thing too, the little blonde I mean. You'd think a man would treat that right, you know? Keep hold of what you've got.'

'You would. Listen, I just need to know where you dropped her. Did it seem like it was her home address?'

'Yeah, it was. We talked. I try and talk to 'em all a bit, you know? I think people expect it these days.'

'I'm sure they do. So where was it you dropped her?'

'She was telling me that it's a bit rough round there. You might be interested, actually. She was saying she could smell weed just about all day from the flat over the corridor, said it was constant like. She said maybe there was someone in there growing the stuff. Could be a good bust for you, that.'

'Yeah, thanks. I'll do the necessary. Now you just need to tell me where you dropped her.'

'Devonshire Road.'

'Devonshire? Don't know it.'

'She don't live actually on Devonshire Road. There's a block of flats at the junction there. I forget the name of the actual road. Trevaine Court, that was it.'

'Trevaine Court. Did you see what flat she went into?'

'Nah. She didn't say either. I saw her go in through the main entrance bit. All the bins are lined up either side. I remember thinking I wouldn't want that outside my place, having to walk past that every day. Like a bin man's guard of honour!'

'That's ideal. Thanks for your help, Colin.' George fished in his pocket and pulled out a crumpled ten pound note. 'For your time. I know I've got in your way today.'

Colin waved it away. 'Nah, you're all right. I don't mind helping you people out. I've called on you a couple of times in the past, and I might have to again one day. Just remember me then, okay?'

'Deal. Good luck with the smoking thing.' George gestured at the e-cigarette.

Colin looked down at it. 'I'm gonna need more than luck, I reckon. A bit of tobacco might do the trick.'

George watched Colin pull away. He pulled his work phone out of his pocket, it had been buzzing in his pocket. Three missed calls from Paul. He considered calling him straight back but decided against it. He would either be after some explanation or looking to continue their argument. Either way he didn't have the time. He needed to get to Trevaine Court right away.

It was in a reasonable part of Dover. The Tower Hamlets area consisted mostly of small, terraced houses in neat rows. Trevaine Court was a block of flats stuck on the end of one of them.

George parked up where he could see the front entrance. He had done a quick recce of the building and this was the only way in or out.

His phone vibrated again with an incoming call. 'Paul, listen, we'll talk later about how this is going to work. Just let me get this done now . . .'

'George Elms.' George recognised the voice at once. It sent a chill coursing through his body. He thought fast. Even though he'd expected contact, this had caught him out.

'Kane Forley. You took your time. I got out days ago.'

'I know.'

'Well, of course you do. You still got your rats scurrying around my building, then?'

'We had this conversation already, George. Seems there's no shortage of people willing to assist for a bit of remuneration.'

'There's nothing you could offer me though, Kane. So why call me? I'll be seeing you soon anyway. The whole world knows we're looking for you.'

'You're right about one thing, George. You will be seeing me soon. You're wrong about me having nothing to offer you though. What about your wife and daughter?'

George looked away from the entrance.

'They're safe. I got them safe. You call *us* predictable, well, I knew you would go after them.'

'Yes, you did. You did a good job too, George. I couldn't find her, and none of my people could either. But I *could* find you. You weren't difficult at all, and you found her, didn't you, George? Stuck something to her car. What was that about, George? Are you having to track your own family now?'

George said nothing.

'They're fine, by the way. But you know how this game plays out. You need to do something for me. Their safety depends on it, etcetera, etcetera. So let's skip the small talk and I'll tell you what I need.'

'You've already got your plans. What I do will make no difference, so don't pretend like it will.' George spoke through gritted teeth. 'You have your issue with me. Just leave my family out of it. We'll meet, on your terms, and you can have your moment.'

'I will have my moment, George. And it's already on my terms.'

George said nothing. He was floundering. Yet again, Kane had him on the back foot. He'd known all along that as long as he could keep his wife and child away from this man, he would have a chance. He no longer cared about anything else. And then he'd led Kane right to them!

'What do you want? What do I do to get my family back?'

'I'm not giving you your family back, George.'

'What do you mean?'

'I'm not just going to hand them back. When you do what I need you to do, I will give you a chance to save them. Just one chance.'

'What are you talking about?'

'You know how I like to keep you guessing, George. That's the fun of this whole thing.'

'I've had just about enough of your games.'

'I'm sure you have. Just one more, George. But lose this last game, and you will lose your family. Just like I lost mine.'

'What do you want from me?'

'Liberty.'

George scowled in confusion. 'What do you mean?'

'Free me, George.'

'Enough of the games, Kane.' But George was talking to a dead handset.

He threw down the phone and lowered his head onto the steering wheel.

The door to the flats opened, and a young woman came through backwards, pulling a buggy. She spun it round and started down the path. George got out of the car and trotted over to her.

'George Elms. I'm a copper from Langthorne.' George did his best to smile, though he felt like weeping.

'What do you want? I told you lot I ain't making no statement.'

George shook his head. 'It's not about you. I'm looking for the Polish girl that lives in your building. Blonde hair, quite petite? Do you know who I mean?'

She shrugged. 'Lot of Slovaks around here.'

'She's Polish.'

'All the fucking same, mate. Oh, her. The one in the first flat on the left, yeah?'

'Yeah, that's it.'

'What do you need to know?'

'Does she live there alone?'

She shook her head. 'I keep myself to myself, you know? We ain't friends like.'

'But you might have seen other people going in and out, or heard them?'

'Young girls mainly. Like thirteen, fourteen. A couple at a time, but always this one girl. Could be the sister. Looks a bit like her.' The young woman frowned.

'Any blokes?'

'I've seen a bloke a couple of times. He's English though.' She was beginning to edge away.

'What did he look like?'

'I don't know. I only know he's English 'cause he held the door for me once, and he said something or other. I didn't really look at him. Couple of days ago, I suppose. Can I go now? I got a meeting with the housing people. They're getting me out of this shithole.'

'Yeah, of course. Thanks for your help.'

With his phone to his ear, George watched her hurry away. It rang and rang, but there was no answer. Paul was playing him at his own game. Voicemail kicked in just as he got into the Skoda.

'Paul, it's George. I was a dick this morning, I know. I do know how you feel. I'm not entirely up with what's going on either, and I'm frustrated. Listen, I can't explain right now but I promise I will. I think Jana's important. I don't quite know how yet, but she might be our leak, or part of it at least. Can you get out to see her as soon as possible? She's in Dover — Trevaine Court on the junction with Devonshire Road. The first flat on the left as you go through the communal. When you're happy she's on her own, try and talk to her. Push her a bit and I'm sure she'll fold. Find out what you can. I gotta go, and I might be offline for a while. I will explain. I'm really sorry, mate. I need you, Paul. There's no one else I trust here now.'

George had been using his work phone. His personal one took two goes with his thumb print to unlock — he was sweating and his hands shook. He called up the GPS device he had attached to Sarah's car. The map appeared on his screen and the red pin landed on Devonshire Road, Dover. George climbed out of the car, phone in hand. He suddenly felt a dread that threatened to consume him. He knelt down and saw at once the flat lump of metal underneath the driver's seat. He pulled it out. It held a folded up piece of paper. The note read, *Free me.*

George rocked back onto his heels, overcome by despair.

Kane Forley had his wife and child.

Chapter 23

The man put his phone back in his pocket and walked up the steps into Langthorne House police station.

The reception area was empty of visitors. Two women sat looking at their computer screens. They didn't look up. After a while one of them called out 'Be with you in a second,' her eyes still on her screen.

'I can wait.' The man wandered around, studying the posters and notices.

The woman who had spoken finally raised her eyes. 'Can I help?'

'There's been a picture on the news. A man you want to talk to about shooting police officers.'

'Oh, right.' The woman looked blank. 'You have some information for us, do you?' She took up a pen.

'The police wish to speak to me.'

'To you? Have you made a report already?' The woman looked puzzled.

'No. I killed nine police officers, including your chief constable. It appears they now know my name. I have come to speak to them on my terms, rather than get picked up off the street like a stray dog. Could you let them know that Kane Forley is here?'

'Kane . . .' She picked up the desk phone, looking suddenly panicked.

'I'll just take a seat.' The man went over to one of the chairs lined up against the wall, and sighed loudly.

Thirty seconds later, two officers burst into the reception area and split into formation. Both carried G36 assault rifles. The lead man moved sideways, his weapon pointed at the seated figure. 'Stay where you are, hands where we can see them. Any movements will be seen as an act of aggression and you will be shot. Do you understand?'

The women from the front counter were being shepherded out.

Kane Forley remained silent. He kept his hands in his lap, palms up. Eventually he raised his head. 'I've interlocked my hands. You can see they are empty, and I will now raise them over my head.'

The lead officer pushed his rifle at him. 'You do what you're told, when you're told!'

Kane smiled. 'I was just trying to help. You seem a little tense. I'm here to talk. If I'd wanted to hurt you, Officer, you would be dead by now.'

'Shut the fuck up! Slowly push your hands in front of you and stand. One movement that I don't like and I will shoot you in the face.'

Kane looked around. 'What? Here? With all the cameras? Go ahead.'

'Stand up slowly,' the officer repeated.

Kane suddenly jumped to his feet, and both police officers started. The man who had given the orders pushed the barrel of his gun into Kane's cheek.

Kane kept on smiling.

'Search him where he is and cuff him. We'll do a thorough search in custody.'

A third officer approached Kane and ran his hands over his shoulders, down his body, and through his pockets. 'Nothing.' The handcuffs snapped shut, and Kane was led out.

The officer's smile was grim. 'You're under arrest for murder.'

* * *

Barry Lance went white when he heard the news. So Kane Forley had handed himself in. What would this mean for him?

He checked the phone that Kane had left for him. No missed calls and no messages. Had Kane Forley seen the news and realised the game was up? What had he done with his wife? Barry guessed she must be dead. What would one more body mean to Kane?

'Baz? Wassup? You okay?'

The acting sergeant found Barry out in the corridor, pacing.

He looked up. 'Oh yeah, I'm cool. I just wanted to be the one to bring him in, you know? It's a bit of an anti-climax like this. It would have been good to kick his door in and drag him here.'

The sergeant shrugged. 'Ah well, he's in clean, no one else is hurt. It can all stop now.'

'Fair point. Well, I should go and see what the deal is. They'll probably want the team to do some searches.'

Barry pushed through the double doors and headed for custody.

* * *

'Boss!' Jim the jailor greeted Barry as he walked into the custody office.

'Bit of a turn up for the books, eh, boss? We've closed custody for now, just while we get him settled in.'

Barry nodded, and swept past Jim to a series of monitors that played video feeds of the cells.

'Cell eleven!' Jim called out.

The monitor showed a figure sitting on a bench facing towards the open cell door. Two officers stood facing him with their backs to the camera. One was seated and the other leant nonchalantly against the door frame. Cells eleven and twelve were intended for juveniles. The doors to these cells were made of reinforced Perspex instead of the harsh steel of the adult cages. This door, and the external toilet, allowed for constant surveillance.

'What did he say at the desk?'

'He's not been booked in yet, boss. It was busy. He's been searched, but the skipper was waiting till the other stuff was dealt with so we could focus on him. Any minute now.'

'Did he have any property on him?'

'No phone, no wallet, nothing. Just a zip bag of white powder. He said it was cocaine.'

'Cocaine?' Barry stared.

'Yup. I mean, who gives themselves up with a bag of coke in their pocket? Anyway, it's not gonna make much difference, is it? He said he forgot.'

'A man like that doesn't forget. I want to stay.'

Jim shrugged. 'No problem. I'll go and find out if we're ready for him.'

* * *

Kane Forley sat in the middle of the bench with his bare feet on the plastic mattress. He had his arms around his legs, and his chin rested on his knees.

He looked up at the overweight jailor.

'The sergeant's going to book you in now.'

Kane put his feet on the floor and went slowly to the custody desk.

'Kane Forley.' The custody sergeant stood up and leaned over the desk to look down at Kane.

'Yes.'

'Do you understand why you have been arrested today?'

'I do. Can you take the cuffs off now, please? I have been searched and I have been absolutely compliant.'

The custody sergeant looked at one of the two officers standing with Kane. The officer nodded and removed the cuffs.

Kane rubbed at his wrists.

'Did you require a solicitor or legal advisor?' asked the sergeant.

'No. But I wish to exercise my right to an eight-hour rest period.'

'Rest period? That's more for people under the influence, or arrested in the middle of the night.'

'I haven't slept. Not for days. Now I'm here and I've got this off my chest, maybe I can sleep. I'm exhausted, too tired to talk to you people yet. I know you've got a lot of questions. And I took cocaine just before I walked in. It helps me function, see?'

The sergeant looked at his watch. 'Eight hours means you won't be spoken to until two this afternoon. If you feel you need to delay—'

'It doesn't delay anything for me now, Sergeant, does it? I mean, I'm not going anywhere, am I? I murdered nine police officers.' Kane stared into the camera above the desk. 'There's your admission. I mean, I'm just going to say the same thing whatever time you speak to me. But I know you're going to want a lot of detail, and I'm so tired.'

'Eight hours rest. And you definitely don't want a solicitor?'

Kane shook his head and grimaced. 'Can you imagine the face of the poor solicitor getting that call? I don't think anyone is going to want to help me now, Sergeant. I'll be fine, thank you.'

'Let me know if you change your mind. You'll have an officer or two just outside your door. It's standard with something as serious as this.'

'Understood.'

The sergeant nodded. 'You can take him to his cell then, please, gentlemen.'

'I'll walk him to his cell.' Kane looked round. A stocky man bearing inspector's pips was standing at the rear of the office.

'Sir?' The sergeant said. The two uniform officers froze.

'I said I will take him.'

'We'll come with you, sir,' offered one of the officers.

'No need. You two might be here for some time. Take the opportunity to get yourselves a cup of tea. Kane, do you want a cup of tea or coffee?'

Kane tilted his head. 'Inspector Lance?'

'Tea or coffee?' said Barry.

Kane smiled broadly. 'Is the coffee any good? Only I have high standards.'

'He'll have a coffee.' The two officers moved off. Barry led Kane a different route back. 'We need to talk,' Barry growled.

Kane walked into cell eleven and turned to face him.

'I have an eight-hour rest period before I need to talk to anyone.'

'Where's my—'

'Inspector!' Kane raised a finger to his lips, and pointed to the camera pointing down at them. 'We don't talk here. If you say something you shouldn't, then it's all over. I think you will understand what that means. You'll need to find somewhere more private. Now, I have an eight-hour rest period and every minute you stand here talking to me is another minute it is being extended.'

The officers returned and bustled in past Barry. Smiling, Kane thanked them. His eyes never once left Barry's face.

Barry turned to leave.

'See you soon!' called Kane.

Chapter 24

Darren Lewis leant on the back of his chair and stared at DCI Lisa Jones. 'So what do we know?' he asked. He had told Barry Lance to sit down, but he was still pacing to and fro.

'He just came in. He made a significant admission to the front counter and custody staff, in front of the cameras. Then he demanded his eight-hour rest period. He doesn't want a solicitor and it looks like he's just waiting to make a full confession.'

'Why the rest period?'

'He said he hadn't been sleeping and he's high on coke. The custody staff weren't convinced he was on anything, but he did have a bag on him. We can't risk interviewing him now, and then have some smart-arse defence lawyer saying he was unfit,' Lisa said.

'Absolutely.' Darren nodded. 'We think this is one of his mind games, right?'

'Of course it is,' Barry snapped.

'It's a fair assumption,' Darren said. 'We know he likes to exercise his power, and show that he knows the way we work. But it suits us too. Gives us more time to prepare.'

Lisa shook her head. 'The way Elms was talking, Forley was going for a big finish of some sort. Giving yourself up and then exercising your right to eight hours' rest is hardly that. There has to be some other reason for delaying us.'

Darren shrugged. 'Maybe. Or maybe he's just looking to run down his clock? He must know that we only have twenty-four hours to question him.'

Lisa shook her head. 'That wouldn't make any sense. We could charge him right now, whether or not he has the eight hours. The interview is a formality really, and if we need to extend his stay there's not going to be any problem getting that sorted.'

'And he didn't give an address?' Darren looked at Barry, who seemed distracted.

Barry paused, mid-stride. 'Er, no, sorry. No, he said NFA. There's nowhere for us to search.'

'Of course he did. So what? We wait till two and see what he says?'

Lisa nodded. 'Seems that way. But that's clearly what he wants. He can still dictate what we do, even here. He's probably getting off on that.'

Darren frowned. 'Well, then maybe we shouldn't? Maybe we should leave him to sweat in his cell for a while. We could get the extension and leave him there till tomorrow morning. Show him that he's on our terms now.'

'Why not? I think we should do whatever we can to show him we're not just going to toe the line. He thinks we're desperate to talk to him. Maybe leaving him with his thoughts will put him on the back foot a bit?' Lisa smiled.

Darren nodded. 'Okay, good. Leave him to rot. This is going to be on our terms now.'

'I'll tell him.' Barry had spoken too eagerly, and the others stared at him.

'I mean, I'll do his custody review. I'll make him aware that he will be interviewed when we're ready, not when he feels like it. I'll let you know how he reacts.'

Darren and Lisa nodded.

Darren stood up. 'Good then. Let's make this piece of shit aware that we're in charge now. And can we keep trying George and Paul? We could really do with them being around.'

Chapter 25

Langthorne town centre was quiet. The working day had started and the shoppers were just beginning to emerge. The couple strolling up the middle of the cobbled high street looked out of place. Both had their heads down. The woman wore a dirty white hoodie with the hood up and pulled tight round her head.

The man shuffled through the dry leaves. He was taller and wore a long, waxed jacket over a white T-shirt. His combat trousers were tucked into heavy boots. He also had his hood up. He had one hand stuck in a pocket, and the other held the lead of a fat Staffordshire bull terrier. Every so often the dog looked up at him hopefully. The man paused once to drink from a can of lager.

The bench at the top of the high street was damp. The man sat down straight away. The woman wiped at the bench with a tissue before she too sat down. The man lit two cigarettes and passed her one.

'What time you gotta go then, Tommy?'

Tommy squinted. 'I was gonna do this fag, then go. You gonna miss me, Weasel?' He patted the dog.

'How long, d'you reckon?'

'You know what they're like, Susan. It'll be like fucking twelve hours or something.'

'Give me your fags and that to look after.'

'Yeah, but I'll want one when I come out.'

Susan rolled her eyes. 'Well, just keep one then, yer dopey cunt.'

'I might want two.'

'How many have we got?' she asked.

'It's a new pack of ten, ain't it? I got it this morning.'

'Take two out and stick 'em in your pocket. You got anything else on you?'

'Nah.'

'You got a lighter?'

'Oh yeah. I'll need that.'

The couple fell silent. Tommy took another swig. An old woman walked past and eyed the can of beer.

'The fuck you looking at, you dopey old bitch?'

The woman looked away and speeded up.

'Fucking people in this town.' Tommy got no response. 'I'm going to McDonalds. You want anything in there?'

'Nah. Have you got money?' Susan looked at him suspiciously.

'You know I ain't, Suze.' He gave her a broad, toothless grin.

'Nah, I'm alright.'

'Back in a minute.'

McDonalds was quiet. The breakfast rush was over, leaving a group of kids in a booth excitedly conversing in French and two women at the counter, both in short leather jackets over leggings. The women were having some difficulty explaining what they wanted. Tommy stopped behind them and swore.

'So where are you ladies from originally?' asked the man behind the counter.

'Romania,' the girls chorused.

'Of course you fucking are.' Tommy said. He gestured with his beer can. 'Ain't no English left in this town no more. You lot coming over here bleeding us dry.'

'Sir, you can't drink that in here. I think you should leave.' Then to the two women, 'I'm sorry about that.'

'What you say? I can't drink this?' Tommy threw the can at the man behind the counter, who ducked. It flew past him and hit the ovens. A second employee emerged from the rear.

'Sir, you need to leave now or I will call the police.'

Tommy smiled. 'Call the fucking police, call them whatever the fuck you like! This place is a shit hole anyway.' Tommy made for the exit. He passed the table where the kids sat watching the goings-on. Tommy scooped up two packets of chips from their table and tipped one into his mouth. He lifted the other in the air.

'Agincourt!' he shouted. The double doors closed behind him.

* * *

Constable John Adams was waiting for a red light to change when the call came in.

'He's wearing a long, dark jacket and camouflage trousers. The male was racially abusive to staff and customers. He stole food then left the shop. The informant said that he was drinking alcohol.'

John rolled his eyes and put his mouth to the radio. 'Understood, control, I'm just round the corner. I'll take a look.'

The McDonalds was just ahead on his right. The lights changed and John got a clear view of a man in a waxed jacket and combats, leaning on the metal railings. He was giving the finger to John's marked police car.

John rounded the corner and parked. He took his time putting on his hat and adjusting it. The man continued to lean on the railings, drinking from a can of beer.

John approached him. 'Do you have some sort of problem?'

'That how you talk to people?'

'It's how I talk to people making obscene gestures at me for no reason.'

'Who says I was?'

'Me.'

The man looked John up and down. 'You're a big fucker, ain't yer? That why you think you can bully people, is it? You making up for when you was in school and the other boys bullied you?'

John smiled broadly. 'If I had a pound for every time I've been told that, I reckon I'd be long retired by now.'

'What about cunt? You ever been called a cunt before?'

The smile dropped. 'You're under arrest.'

'Am I now? What's that for then? Having an opinion?'

'No. Theft.'

The man stepped towards him. 'What have I nicked then?'

John took out his cuffs.

'Food,' he said. He reached for the man's arm.

'Well, that's a fucking shit thing to get nicked for, ain't it?' The man stepped back and pushed the can into John's face. The blow struck John's nose, but he came roaring back. He hit the man hard in the abdomen, winding him. He fell to the floor, gasping like a landed fish. John snapped the cuffs on, wiped the beer off his face and radioed for a van.

There was no way this beer-soaked piece of shit was sitting in the back of *his* car.

* * *

The Mercedes Sprinter van arrived with its lights spinning, just minutes after John's call. Tommy was flung into the back, where he missed the bench and fell to the floor. The cage doors slammed shut and Tommy struggled to his feet. The officer who'd nicked him spoke through the mesh.

'My colleague here knows you, Tommy Wilkes. You're on a court order not to be drinking in a public place.'

'I don't know what you're talking about. I need a piss.'

'I think you do know, Tommy. It doesn't matter anyway. You're also under arrest for assaulting a policeman. The time is 09.30.' The officer wrote this down in his notebook.

'I need a fucking piss!'

'You're an adult. We're five minutes from Langthorne custody.'

'I need a piss now!'

'You've got a cheek, haven't you? You punch me in the face and then you expect me to help you out?'

'I don't give a fuck. I'll piss right here then.'

The officer sighed. 'Then you'll be charged with criminal damage as well.'

Tommy Wilkes laughed. He was still laughing when he pulled his penis out. He made sure he got a good amount on his own trousers.

The rear doors slammed shut, there was a bang on the side and the van pulled away.

Chapter 26

'It isn't an interview I want, Inspector Lance.' Kane cocked his head, as if he were studying the man standing over him. The two uniforms were on either side, stiff as bookends.

'I did want to talk to you but like I said, in private.'

Barry turned to the uniforms. 'I'll speak to the prisoner in the consultation room. You can wait outside.'

The officer stared at Barry. 'Sir?'

'Like I said, you can wait outside. I'll know where you are if I need you.'

The two officers still hesitated. 'We'll get a cup of coffee then. Do you want one, sir?'

'No thank you.'

Kane stood up. 'Me neither. The coffee is just as bad as I expected.'

The consultation room was tiny. Barry and Kane stood facing each other with very little space between them.

The door clicked shut, and Barry began at once. 'Where's my wife? And you'd better make it quick because I'm starting to run very low on patience.'

'Listen, Inspector Lance. Your wife is fine, but her safety is very much linked to mine. Do you understand?'

'What do you mean?'

'George Elms is what I mean.'

Barry was taken aback. 'What does he have to do with it?'

'He's not planning on me making it out of here alive.'

'What are you talking about?'

'I talked to him and he made it quite clear. He told me he was getting me out of here so he could deliver justice his own way. I think we both know what that means, Inspector.'

'Don't be ridiculous.'

'Look, I came here to put an end to it all. Once you people worked out who I was, I knew it was all over. I couldn't cope with being hunted like a dog, waiting for you lot to come kick my door in. I knew it was just a matter of time. I was going to use your wife as leverage to get away from here and find out what you knew. I thought maybe you could keep the investigation away from me, but I ran out of time. I knew that if I waited for you to arrest me I'd most likely get hurt, so I came in. I admitted everything in front of your cameras. I don't want any more stress. You can have your wife back, and I mean that. I just want this over.'

'Fine. So tell me where she is.'

'It doesn't work like that, Barry. I need to make it to prison. It's not such a bad option. I'll be a bit of a legend in there, and there's nothing left for me on the outside.'

Barry looked at him. 'A legend? Is that what you think?'

'I know it. We both know criminals, Barry. A cop killer, nine times over!' Kane's eyes suddenly widened. 'I had you people on the ropes. That will be known on the inside. I'll be looked after, maybe even feared.'

'Believe what you want.' Barry shook his head.

'Just get me to prison. The second I walk in, I get my rights to a phone call, and you're it. She's fine now, but she's not a well woman, Barry. If she's left alone for much longer, she *will* die.'

Barry lunged forward and pinned Kane against the wall.

'You can kill me,' gasped Kane, 'but you'll kill your wife too.'

'Where is she?' Barry's grip tightened.

'I'll tell you.'

Barry let go and stepped back.

Kane took a few moments to recover. 'Get me into prison. Keep that psycho away from me, and you have my word I will give you what you need to save Shelley's life.'

'Your word? What fucking good is your word?'

'It's all you have.'

Chapter 27

Helen Webb was lying on the ground in the corner of the dark warehouse in her filthy underwear. The chair had gone and so had the chains. She touched her head gingerly. She had expected to be interrogated, but instead was beaten until she lost consciousness. Several times. She was hungry, and her throat was dry. Her face and ribs hurt the most. From where she lay, she could see the door through which her tormentor came and went. They were using a tactic she was only too familiar with — a little kindness, a promise of release, followed by a senseless beating. Knowing what they were doing didn't help her, though. Helen was resigned to dying here.

She heard a footstep behind her but didn't have the energy to lift her head to look. She screwed her eyes tight shut and tried to think of her twin daughters. All she wanted was to see them once more, and say goodbye. The footsteps drew closer. She could feel his breath against her cheek.

'Helen Webb. You are under arrest.'

Now what were they up to? A new game and a different voice, someone she hadn't heard before. She tried to turn and groaned.

'Don't try to move. How badly hurt are you?'

'I don't know.' It came out as a whimper, which made her angry — she was stronger than that.

'Where are they?' he said.

'Who?'

'The men who did this?'

'I don't know. It's been just one, mainly. He comes from there.' Helen pointed towards the door. She tried to sit and felt his hands in her armpits, pulling her up. The man stepped back and looked around.

He spoke in a harsh whisper. 'Can you walk?'

'I think so.'

He nodded, and looked around. He appeared to be searching for something. The chain that had been used to restrain Helen lay in a pile beside the door. The man walked towards it.

'Get to your feet.'

The man went to the door and put his ear against it. Then he stepped into the shadows, out of sight. Helen tried to move and decided that the pain was mostly stiffness and bruising. Her face was swollen, one of her eyes was half closed and two teeth were loose. Flexing her bruised muscles was agony.

'Are you bad?' The man padded back and squatted beside her, looking concerned.

'I don't think so.'

'You look bad.'

'Thanks. Nothing's broken. I think it's just bruising.'

'We have to get going. I don't know how much time we have.'

'Who are you?' Helen pushed at the hair stuck to her sweaty forehead.

'I'm a police officer. I've been working undercover in one of Alcani's crews. You can call me Mick.'

'You're police? Here? I had no idea we were still . . . you know.'

'Not many do. After the last operation they had the grand idea of having me stay on. They figured the family wouldn't think we'd leave any coppers here after that.'

'Sounds risky.' Helen was dubious.

'Tell me about it. Look, we need to get going.'

'Going where?' Helen tried bending her legs. They seemed to be working.

'Custody. Unless you'd rather stay here?'

Helen put her weight on her legs, which trembled. 'You know who I am then?'

'I know who you are,' Mick said, 'and I know what you did.'

'So why not leave me here? You're putting yourself at enormous risk. These people won't think twice—'

'I know all about these people. You need to face up to what you did, and who you did it to. But not like this.'

Suddenly the door opened. Mick reacted instantly, and merged into the shadows. The man at the door looked at Helen standing in front of him.

'Where the fuck have you been?' she snarled. 'I've been waiting for you to come back and finish me off. Unless you can't manage it on your own!'

The man grunted. He stepped towards her, his hands bunched, ready to strike. With a faint chinking sound, Mick slipped the chain deftly over his head. He pulled it tight around the man's throat. The man scrabbled at the cold metal until all movement ceased and Mick let him drop to the ground.

'He's dead.' Mick's voice held shock.

'Good.' Helen looked about her until she spotted a pile of rags flung into a corner. She dug out her hooded top. Her boots were underneath, but she couldn't find her trousers.

'We have to go!' Mick called out.

'I can't find my trousers.'

'Put on anything. I just killed a man. We can't wait.' Mick had already turned away.

'Dammit.' Helen stumbled after him, her face contorted in pain.

Chapter 28

Mick had made her sit in the rear of the van. He was in a hurry. Thrown about against the hard wooden benches, Helen groaned.

Mick almost reached the gate before he was forced to stop.

'Keep your head down,' he said through clenched teeth. Danesh Alcani was strolling out of the Portakabin with his arm raised. Mick took a deep breath and rolled his window down.

'Mr Alcani.' Mick did his best to sound cheery. 'You having a better day today?'

'Always a good day here, Mick.'

Meek. Why did he have to do it? 'What can I do for you? You got your money from the other night, right?'

Danesh leant on the window frame and peered into the cab. The seat backs blocked any view of the back.

'I got my money. I always get my money. What brings you back here today, Mick? I didn't get a call.'

'Really? Sorry. We're looking at another job. We might need something with a bit more bite for this one, a bit more industrial, you know? I was seeing what's available and how portable it might be.'

'Did you find what you need?'

'I saw some possibles.'

'Did you take them, Mick?' Danesh glared at him.

'Is there something wrong?'

'Yeah. There is something wrong, Mick. Seems we've had some stuff go missing from the site. Some tools, heavy cutting equipment. The sort of stuff you might be talking about, as a matter of fact.'

'You think someone's stealing from you? From Alcani's yard? You'd have to be pretty fucking stupid to do that, Danesh. I ain't that stupid.'

'Pop the back of the van, will you, Mick?' Danesh stepped back and nodded. A second man walked towards the rear of the van and pulled at the doors. They were locked.

Mick left the engine running. He jumped out and strode to the rear of the van.

'What the fuck is all this about? You accusing me of stealing?'

'When I ask you to open your van, you open your fucking van. You remember who you work for, Mick, or I'll have to find a way of reminding you.'

'Do it then. Find a way. I don't work for you, that's for fucking sure. You're just the man who answers the phone. You think you can strut around, accusing *me* of stealing your shit? I give your family forty grand for one night's work and then you accuse me of stealing — what? Some tools?'

'Back the fuck down, Mick, or you'll be backed down permanently.'

'Do it then. Fucking do it. You and your man here, if you can't manage it by yourself.'

Danesh took a step forward and Mick readied himself for the blow. Then he heard a voice.

'Danesh! What the fuck's going on here?' Sol Alcani strode towards them.

'There's a problem. This fucker thinks he can get up in my face. Thinks he don't need to follow instructions when he's on my site.'

'This ain't your site.' Sol turned away from his brother and faced Mick. 'What's the problem here?'

'I didn't have no problem. I work one of your cash crews. We did a job just last night — earned you forty grand. We've got our eye out for another, but it's gonna need some more equipment. I was just seeing what you've got.'

'You find what you was looking for?'

'Possibly. It depends on whether you can move your sheet metal cutting machine.'

Sol shook his head. 'It's not meant to be moved, and even if you could, you'd have a problem powering the thing. It's not your standard plug.'

'I thought that. I was going back to the snatch site, to see what can be done. I don't like to give up easy.'

Sol smiled. 'I respect that. I heard about the cash-snatch job. Sounds like it was a good, clean job.'

'It went well. It was planned to go well, and it did.'

'You would have been up all night too and here you are, back on the next job. What's your name?'

'Mick.'

'Well, Mick, how did you go from showing my family the respect of a forty-thousand-pound deposit to fronting up my brother on our turf?' Sol's eyes narrowed.

'Respect is a two way thing. At least, that's the way I see it. I did what I needed to and I was on my way back to the snatch site. I'm grafting for both you and me here. Your brother here stops me and starts accusing me of stealing your stuff. Okay I'm a thief, but I choose who I steal from and I wouldn't choose you.'

Sol turned back to his brother. 'That's what this is all about?'

'Tools are going missing. Started small but we're losing expensive shit now — cutters, generators and such.'

'Brother, do you know how many thieves, liars and general criminals we get through these gates every single day?'

'It's disrespectful.'

'It is. And we will find out who it is, and then you'll get the opportunity to personally cut their hands off. But we can't push one of our best partners around!'

'It ain't personal. I been checking loads.'

Sol turned back to Mick and rolled his eyes. 'It ain't personal, he's been checking loads. So let's teach my brother here a lesson. Let's open the back of the van, prove you're innocent and justifiably outraged, and then we can all get on with our lives.'

'You still want me to open the doors?' Mick said. His voice faltered.

'Well, yeah. Then it's all over, isn't it?'

Mick went back to the cab and pulled the keys from the ignition. He walked towards the rear door. He slid the key into the lock, twisted the handle, took a deep breath and pulled it open.

Mick stepped aside. The gate was two hundred metres away. He'd never make it.

'There you are, see? Not our man. Are you happy now, Danesh?'

Danesh was already walking away. Mick peered inside at the empty benches. The empty interior.

'Nothing personal you understand, Mick. My brother doesn't understand the priorities. That was good work last night. We need good men like you around.'

'Yeah. Sounds like you got a bit of a thief problem. Good luck with that.'

Mick walked back to the driver's door and pulled it open. Helen Webb lay curled up in a foetal position in the passenger side foot well. Her wide, panicked eyes met Mick's.

'Oh, and Mick?'

Sol was directly behind him. Mick turned, pushing the door to behind him.

'Wassup?' Mick replied.

'If we don't have what you need here, come and see me. I can sometimes source equipment from elsewhere, if you know what I mean? If it's worth the effort.'

Mick nodded. 'Double the last haul, I reckon. I'd go to a lot of effort for that sort of return.'

Sol smiled again and held out his hand. 'Man after my own heart.'

Chapter 29

George marched back into Langthorne House just as two uniform officers were on their way out. The first officer held the door for him. Her colleague scowled and made a comment. George ignored it. He ignored his phone too. He guessed it would be Paul, still trying to get some clarity. Right now, George couldn't give him any. He had never been more bewildered. And guilty. He had led the very man he was trying to keep away from them right to his wife and child. He hadn't even made it difficult. George touched the piece of paper he had hurriedly stuffed into his pocket. *Free me.* George had no idea what it meant.

He pulled his personal phone out of his pocket. Seven missed calls. Two were from Paul as he had expected, and the rest were from Darren Lewis.

When he got to his office, Darren Lewis was coming out. He greeted George with a beaming smile.

'You've heard then? I tried to let you know.'

'Heard what?'

'Kane Forley. He's in the bin.'

George tried on a few expressions. None seemed appropriate.

'When? How did we find him?'

'We didn't. He walked in and gave himself up! Made some significant comments to the front counter staff — they're giving statements as we speak — then again at the custody desk. He's clearly in the mood to cough to what he did and go to prison, and we're certainly happy to help him with that.'

'He just walked in?'

'Yup. Just after eight this morning. He's downstairs.'

'Was that all he said? Did he say anything in custody?'

'He's demanded his rest period. Said he didn't sleep a wink last night with all the guilt weighing on his mind, or some such rubbish. Said he was high on coke too, so we do need to play the game. He seems to be expecting us down there at two on the dot. I think we'll let him sweat in there for a bit longer. I guess this is all part of him trying to control his environment, like you said?'

George nodded. Slowly. His eyes were unfocused. 'Yeah, that's what it will be.'

'You okay, George? I expected a different reaction from you. This means it's over for you.'

George shook his head. 'Yeah, I'm fine. I just can't quite believe it. I guess we need to prep for the interview. I mean, there's a lot of work to do.'

'Don't you worry about that. We've got an interview team already doing their homework. It will take a few days, I imagine. I've got the DCI for Major Crime leading it. They're already talking about extensions.'

'Do you need me to do anything?' asked George.

'You can speak to the team. I'd appreciate that. Do you think Kane will be expecting you to interview him?'

'No. He's clever enough to know that it can't be me. He'd probably like me to, though. It would give him another opportunity to play his games. They will need to keep to the facts. They can't let him dictate how it goes. He will be difficult, I'm sure. I can't see him just coming in and deciding to play ball after all that's gone on.'

Darren nodded. 'I agree. I certainly think they would benefit from speaking to you. You can at least give them some idea of what to expect. But he's in, that's what matters. It almost doesn't matter too much what he says. We have his DNA. Finally he's under our control. He won't be able to lead us now.'

George watched Darren go. Then he went over to a window, leant against the sill and gazed down at the people going about their business below. Panic began to well up inside him. Kane Forley was in custody downstairs, something George had become consumed with making happen. And now he knew for certain what he had to do to ensure the safety of his wife and child.

Free me.

Chapter 30

'George Elms! Well, I never thought I'd see you again.' Jim the jailer had a big, open smile. 'I always said it was rubbish.'

'I'll never forget the tea you made me.' George smiled back, remembering how Jim had broken ranks and treated him kindly when he was on the wrong side of one of these cell doors.

George took in the screens lined up along one wall. The camera system had been upgraded since he'd last been in, and now it was all in high definition.

Jim had said something.

'Sorry?'

'I take it you're down here about Forley? He's in the juvenile bit so we can keep an eye on him easy, and keep him away from the rest.'

'Oh right, yeah.' George looked again at the monitors. The figure in number eleven had a blue custody issue blanket wrapped around him. He seemed very alone, almost vulnerable. George knew better. Kane Forley had never been more in control.

'Are you speaking to him?' asked Jim.

'The skipper will probably get the hump if I do,' George replied, his throat suddenly dry.

Jim shrugged. 'To be honest, I think Matt expected you down here earlier. I don't think he'd have any issue with a little gloating. Just don't get your hands round his neck or I'll have to pile in and hit you with the cut-down kit!' Jim laughed.

George managed to smile. 'No promises.' He stepped forward just as Matt Dobson, the custody sergeant, came in through the swinging doors. His response was similar to Jim's.

'George Elms! Nice to have you back, mate. What brings you down here?' The smile on Matt's face suddenly dropped away. 'You know some DCI spoke to me? She warned me to keep you away. Seems they're worried you might come down here and cause trouble. That's not why you're here, is it?'

'Of course not, Matt. Like I would cause any trouble.'

'Good. Then I will be very busy for the next three minutes. There's a lot going on down here. Just don't do anything I might notice.'

'Understood.' George had been lucky. Matt Dobson was the most laid back custody sergeant he'd ever worked with, and he was an old friend.

* * *

The two officers with Kane Forley were watching him approach. George saw them exchange glances as he drew near.

One of them greeted him. George noticed the clipboard with the prisoner's custody record on it. He could see from this officer's force number that he was brand new. He would have drawn the short straw and was stuck with supervision duty.

'This isn't an official visit, so you don't need to record it.' The two officers exchanged another look and George smiled at them. 'I'll write down anything significant.'

The officer handed him the clipboard.

George looked at the officers. 'I need to speak to the prisoner.'

Neither officer made a move. 'We've been told not to leave him alone,' said one.

'He won't be alone, will he? He'll be with me.'

The new officer shook his head. 'Two at all times, that's what the skipper said.'

'Well, if you could just wait round the corner. If I need someone to hold my hand, I can call.'

'Sorry, Sarge, I didn't mean to—'

'Don't be sorry. You're right to ask. I'll just be a minute.'

The other officer stretched and got to his feet. 'Come on, Tone. Let's go get a cup of tea while we have the chance.'

George waited for them to leave.

Kane had been watching the exchange with an amused expression. 'How have you been?' he said.

'I don't have time for pleasantries,' George spat out.

Kane smiled. 'There's always time to be pleasant.'

'What do you want from me?'

'What time is it?' asked Kane.

'Around midday.'

'Midday? So there is time after all. We need to be away from here at two this afternoon. There's a very strict schedule.' Kane yawned, he carried himself like they might have been making arrangements for a lazy lunch.

George looked at him. 'What happens at two?'

'Nothing, but we will need to get a move on, George. Like I said, there's a tight schedule.'

'It's not possible. You think I can just come down here at two o'clock when your rest period ends and all eyes are on you — and then what? Walk you out?'

'I thought I might attract some interest.' Kane seemed pleased at the thought.

'Why turn yourself in if you just want me to lead you back out again? I'm done with your games. We all are.'

'I thought you would be. That's why I took your wife and child. It was a lot of work, but I needed to be sure you'd play your part.'

'This is your final play though, right? You're not going to let my family live. Why would you? What do you have to gain from it?'

'You're right, George. There's nothing to gain from them living. But there is everything to gain from watching you try. You will try, because there's still a chance you can save them. You'll see what I mean. When you get me out of here, I'll take you to where they're currently sitting — on top of a rather crude lump of explosive. Amazing what you can learn from the internet these days.'

'Jesus, Kane. She's seven years old! Your issue is with me.'

'Your issue was with my brother. Didn't stop you wiping out my whole family though, did it?'

'Your brother killed himself. That killed your mum because she couldn't stand the shame of what he was. What do you think she'd make of what *you* are?'

Kane's expression hardened. 'If someone had given me the chance to save her, I would have done everything I could. I would have done *anything* I could. We're no different. You need to be here at two. We'll need a car, and we need to get away clean.'

George snorted. 'How the fuck do you think I'm going to manage that?'

'You're going to have to do some of the thinking yourself, George, but I can offer you some assistance. Tommy Wilkes should be in by now. Find out where. When you need the focus off me, bang on his cell door three times. He'll do the rest.'

George knew the name. 'Tommy Wilkes? He's some town drunk, isn't he?'

'He's perfect for what we need. He was cheap too.'

The two uniform officers appeared at the door, clutching steaming paper cups.

'Have you had long enough, Sarge?'

'Yeah, thanks.' George walked away.

On his way out, George greeted Matt, and then checked the board displaying the prisoners' names. Cell three showed *Tommy Wilkes — Theft — Contagious.*

Chapter 31

'You gonna tell me your story then?'

'I'm under caution, right? Anything I say and all that?' Helen Webb had waited nearly ten minutes before getting up from the floor. The drive out of the compound was torture. The stiff suspension bounced them over the rutted track, and she groaned at each jolt. Finally she was able to sit up. She expelled a long sigh and put her head back against the headrest.

'Well, I'm hardly in a position to write down what you say, am I? We've got some time to kill, so we might as well talk.'

'I thought you were driving me to the nearest police station. If you like a bit of drama, you could walk me into the chief constable's office. It'd be the defining moment of your career.' Her eyes closed. She had never been so exhausted.

'Not my style. I'm meeting my handler tonight. I figured I'd take you along and make you her problem. I know the Alcanis have quite a reach, so it's risky to just walk you into a police station. If I take you to my handler, she'll understand that she really does need to make me disappear. That's *my* defining moment.'

Helen smiled. 'Ah yes. Disappearing. It's a lovely thought, isn't it?'

'Was that your plan? Where did the Alcanis come in?'

Helen opened her eyes. 'I got desperate. I went to them with an offer. I had managed to stay off the radar for a few weeks, but then I saw the news that George Elms got released. I figured George would put a new emphasis on the search.'

'What makes you think they weren't trying before George was released?' he asked.

'They didn't even do the basics. I was able to use my bank accounts for a few days. There's been no press release. I could speak to my mum, and no one had spoken to her. She didn't even know I was wanted.' Helen shrugged.

'Did you tell her?'

'No, I didn't tell her. I thought about it, but I couldn't think how to say it.'

Mick frowned. 'Why wouldn't they look for you?'

'They will. I'm a big embarrassment. I guess they might be trying to get their house in order before I become their next public mistake. They've got a cop killer to find.'

'Your mate you mean. Maybe you could help out with that?'

'What do you think I did?'

He shook his head. 'It doesn't matter what I think.'

Helen gazed out of the window. 'So where are you taking me?'

'We need to get you some new clothes. And I guess you might want something to eat?'

Helen looked down. Her hooded top was filthy, and her legs were streaked with grime. She had open wounds on her elbows and knees and dried blood on her face. 'I would do just about anything for a hot bath, but yeah, I do need to eat. What did you have in mind?'

'Well, a Tesco or something, with a clothes aisle and a café. You could have a wash in the sink in the bathroom.'

Helen laughed. 'You're going to walk me into Tesco looking like this? In my underwear? I thought you wanted to blend in until we meet your friend tonight. Far be it from me to tell you how to do your job, but your idea stinks.'

Mick scratched his chin. 'Okay. Plan B then.' He pulled his phone out of his pocket and glanced down at it. 'Firstly we need to get somewhere with a fucking signal.'

'You need to make a call?'

'Well, yeah, I do now. Seems like I need to speak to someone about running a bath. I need to speak to my handler too, so she knows you're coming along.'

Helen closed her eyes. She leant back in her seat and finally succumbed to her exhaustion.

Chapter 32

George hardly noticed the three men and two women, with their faces turned expectantly towards him. They looked like detectives, all suits, ties and stress lines.

One of them was Darren Lewis. 'George, thanks for coming up. This is the interview team from Major Crime. We're just discussing tactics. What can you tell these people?'

Skipping the introductions, George launched ahead. 'Where are you with the interviews? Are you planning on talking to him as soon as his rest period runs out?'

Darren shook his head. 'No. He's clearly trying to dictate terms to us, so we'll make him wait a few hours. We'll start by hitting him with the facts, and then we'll bed him down so he gets all night to stew on what we know. There's a lot of evidence.'

'I assume you're looking to extend his stay here, then?' George asked.

'Yes. Prison will be a relative luxury compared to the four bare walls downstairs.'

George frowned. 'I'm not sure I'd call it a luxury.'

Darren looked embarrassed. 'Poor choice of words.'

George waved a hand and Darren said, 'Well, he can stay here until the very last minute. We're not going to have a problem getting a charge when we need it.'

'That is true.'

'So what's his play here, George? Has he just come in to put his hand up for what he's done? Is it all over now?'

George shook his head. 'No. I mean, we still don't know where he's been staying. You need to be putting every resource into finding that out, sir. With respect, we could do with knowing where it is prior to interview.' George tried not to sound too eager.

Darren smiled, and George immediately knew that he was holding something back.

Darren leaned forward and fidgeted with one of the coffee cups. The others followed suit. George restrained himself from grabbing the chief by the scruff of his neck and shaking him.

Finally Darren spoke. 'We have found *something* by going through the land registry. It's just a garage registered to Forley, but it's a place to start—'

'I assume you are planning on searching that sooner rather than later?' George cut in. His pulse began to race.

'Barry Lance and his team are already on their way with a warrant. At least we can gain entry and an initial assessment. See if there's anything that we can ask about in the interview.'

George sat forward. 'Maybe I should go along? They need to be careful, you know. I mean, this could all be part of his next move. Do they know to be careful? A booby trap would be just his style.' He could hear himself begin to babble.

'It'll be fine, George. Barry Lance is just about the most experienced man we have. And with the greatest of respect, I'm not sure you would be welcome. I'll make sure you get updated as soon as I hear.'

The quickening of his pulse had set off his tinnitus. One of the female officers asked a question he almost missed. 'What do you expect from him in interview, George?'

He took a second before replying. 'I expect him to enjoy every minute of it. He's an extremely arrogant man who thinks he's very clever. I think he will talk to you willingly. You'll need to feed his ego a little. I would play dumb, be impressed with how clever he has been. I wouldn't reveal what we know too early on.'

She scribbled some notes. 'Makes sense.'

'Are you aware of his back story?' George asked. 'Of his motive for the whole thing? What happened to his brother and his mum?'

She nodded. 'Darren filled us in with what you told him. I spoke to Paul Baern as well. He was involved in the William Forley case, and some of the fallout from it.'

'I have no doubt he will bring that up, but my advice would be to let him do that in his own time. It's very emotive for him, and it could easily make him angry to the point where he stops giving us what we need.'

'Good advice,' Darren said.

George pushed back his chair. 'Boss, is there anything more you need from me? I was hoping to get back to trying to find out where he's been all this time.'

Darren looked around. 'People? Anything more we need from George here?'

They shook their heads, and George almost ran from the room.

Chapter 33

Barry Lance sized up the garage door, aware of his colleagues watching him. His tension was obvious to everyone. He'd been behaving oddly for some time now. He'd almost had a full-blown argument with Darren Lewis when Darren had asked him to head up the search. At first he had refused to leave the station. Then he had thought about what might be behind the door and rushed his team so that they had been forced to leave some of the door-entry kit behind, the more subtle tools that weren't immediately to hand. Barry insisted on taking a separate vehicle for himself. He had followed them out of Langthorne House in an unmarked black BMW 4x4.

There was no way to see inside the locked garage, and this did nothing to improve his mood. Barry ran his gloved hand over the rusty metal. The only part of the door that looked cared for was the lock, which had evidently been fitted recently.

Barry pushed at the top of the door. Nothing happened. He put his hand on the lock and looked over his shoulder at the men just behind him. They took the hint and stepped back.

'You should get further back than that,' Barry growled.

'There's no need, boss. Just wait for the dog.' A particle-detection dog was on its way. It would be able to nose out any explosive device inside.

'We don't have time to be waiting for the fucking dog.' Barry tightened his fingers around the lock. The men withdrew.

'Locked,' Barry grunted. 'Halton! Bring the drill.'

The drill whined and pushed through the lock. Barry twisted the handle and at the same time, pushed at the top of the door.

The garage was empty, the floor streaked with fresh brush marks.

'Hello, what's this?' One of Barry's colleagues was looking up into the exposed rafters, where the door rested parallel to the roof. He pulled at a long, yellow piece of Perspex balanced on one of the beams.

'A number plate,' Barry said.

'For a bike.' Another of the men radioed control with the number.

The check took seconds. *'Can confirm it is a Yamaha FZX 750 Fazer. Currently showing SORN. No insurance either, but there are keeper details.'*

'Go ahead.'

'Edward Forley of flat 5, Churchill House, Romney Avenue, Langthorne.'

'Edward Forley,' repeated Barry.

'Sounds like we need to do another search, boss. I'll write it up for your signature.'

Barry sighed. He was desperate to get back to the station, but he couldn't tell his men why.

'Yeah,' he said. 'Let's get it done now.'

Chapter 34

Churchill House stood on a patch of bare ground, foursquare and solid. It was not an attractive building, though some of the residents had made an effort to brighten the forbidding exterior with hanging plants and welcome mats. The team soon found flat five on the ground floor. Barry peered in through the front window and made out a kitchen sink, work surface and units, and a half-empty bottle of washing-up liquid. It looked clean, tidy and sparse.

Barry hammered on the door. Sam Halton had bought the enforcer, but the team was reluctant to use it, afraid the door might be rigged.

But Barry couldn't wait. 'We'll have to force it.'

Ryan Dobson, Barry's second in command, looked doubtful. 'We left the lock-pick kit back at the nick, but it's not too far. It would give us a far more controlled entry.'

'We don't have the time to be fucking about!' Barry shook his head. 'Sorry, Dobbo, I'm under pressure here. The acting chief wants a phone call and I need to get back.'

‘It wouldn’t take long to drill it out and snap the lock.’ Ryan raised his eyebrows.

‘Fine, but we’ll have the enforcer to hand.’

‘Understood. We’ll be through that door in minutes. Then you can head back if you want to. We can handle this.’

Ryan probably wanted him out of the way, and Barry couldn’t blame him. He wasn’t an easy man to work with at the moment.

Ryan pushed the drill into the centre of the lock but it laboured and stopped. This was not going to work.

‘I don’t understand it,’ Ryan complained. ‘We’ll have to pick it.’

‘No time.’ Barry growled. ‘I’ve only ever seen a drill fail on a reinforced lock. It won’t pick either. Take the fucking door off.’

Barry nodded at Sam Halton. Sam looked at Ryan, who shrugged.

‘I’ll brace.’ Lee Howiss sat down in front of the door, leaned back, placed the soles of his boots against it, and pushed.

Barry’s phone rang. He swore loudly and paced away from the flat at a distance where he could concentrate on the call.

‘Barry, how are you getting on?’ asked Darren Lewis.

‘No answer at the address. We’re just about to gain entry.’

‘Okay, good. I got the update about the garage. This is the only link we have to him, Barry. We really need something.’

Barry opened his mouth to reply when he heard the blast.

‘What was that, Barry?’

Barry snatched to the sound, smoke and dust suddenly swept towards him along the walkway.

‘It was an explosion! Jesus it was an explosion! Send help!’

'A what? Barry! Are you all okay?'

Barry cut the call and made his way back towards flat five.

Chapter 35

Tommy Wilkes really hated being sober.

A cup of very sweet coffee was passed to him through the hatch. He took it and stuck two fingers up at the cell door. Maybe four sugars would compensate for the lack of alcohol. It didn't. He sat at the end of his bed, some distance from the microwave meal sitting half-eaten on the floor. He knew what he had to do. He just wanted to get on with it now.

And there it was. Three slaps on the outside of his door. Tommy took another swig of his coffee. Time to get started.

Tommy lay on his bed, under a flimsy cover, facing into the camera in the opposite corner. He pushed a hand under his waistband and felt for his anus. It was slightly bulbous and tender to the touch. The package was just under the surface. It was uncomfortable easing it out, but not half as bad as getting it in. That bit never got easier.

Tommy had the package free in less than a minute. He rolled over to face the wall and picked at the wrapping. He freed the two razor blades, concealed them in his fist and sat up. He would finish his coffee first. He was damned sure he wouldn't be getting offered another any time soon.

* * *

George made it to the kitchen. The two officers still watching Kane Forley hadn't seen him. They both looked bored, and were tapping idly at their smart phones. To George's relief, the kitchen area was empty. Now he had to wait, with no real idea what for. He was on tenterhooks. So much was riding on the next few moments, and so much could go wrong. His ears buzzed, and his tinnitus thudded to the beat of his heart. He pushed the door open slightly so he could hear any noises coming from outside. He was a long way from cell three.

An alarm suddenly ripped through the busy custody area, and everyone stood still. George knew it would bellow out across the building, summoning every able officer to the depths of the station.

George emerged slowly from the kitchen and peered along the corridor. The two men guarding Kane Forley were on their feet, both watching the custody desk.

'Knife!' The shout came from the corridor on the other side of the floor. The block was suddenly a melee of running feet and raised voices. One of the officers broke away from his post. The other stood looking into Kane's cell.

George made his move. He walked up behind the officer and spoke into his ear, making him jump.

'Jesus! The fella round there's got a knife! You go help. I'll stand guard on him.' George pointed at the wide-eyed officer's chest. 'You've got the vest on.' The officer hurriedly zipped up his stab vest, nodded at George and was gone.

Kane Forley got to his feet and shook his legs.

'We going, then?' Kane asked.

'Just do as I say.'

* * *

Barry ran to the flat. Smoke swirled out the door, and a ferocious heat came with it. His team stumbled about, rubbing their eyes. No one seemed to be seriously injured and all were accounted for. Through the acrid smog, Barry noticed an orange glow. He acted quickly. He threw himself through the doorway and was able to dash into the kitchen, away from the smoke that was being funnelled through the open door. He searched round frantically until he found the fire. A small sofa sat burning in the centre of the open-plan flat. Someone was sitting there, still upright and now almost entirely engulfed in flames. Barry saw the blue jeans. A black and white headscarf. A white T-shirt, melting in the intense heat. It had a large black YSL emblem on the front.

Oh God, no.

'Shelley!' Barry shrieked, sucked in a lungful of black smoke and coughed. He looked around wildly and saw a beach towel hanging over the radiator in the kitchen. Barry threw it into the sink and ran water over it. He threw the soaked towel over the burning figure. It put out the fire but Barry was blinded by smoke. He grabbed at the figure and his hands immediately stuck to it. He pulled back, his fingers covered in melting plastic. The dummy pitched forward. Barry turned away and ran out of the flat.

Outside, Barry collapsed, gasping. Ryan got to him first and pulled him to his feet.

'Barry! You okay?'

'My hands!'

Ryan looked at the blackened fingers. 'Jesus, what happened?'

'It wasn't her,' Barry said, his eyes still shut. 'It wasn't her!'

'Who, Barry? You're okay, mate. We'll get the burns kit.'

'It wasn't anyone.' Tears streamed from Barry's eyes. Ryan thought it was the smoke.

* * *

Barry doused his hands in cold water and then applied a specialist burn cream. One of the team had wrapped bandages tightly round them, but he could still use them a little. He sat on the ground with Ryan beside him. The team had retrieved some bottles of water from the van. Ryan was opening and closing his jaw to clear the ringing in his ears. All the officers were covered in soot. Barry's phone had been ringing incessantly. He finally felt able to answer it.

'Boss?'

'Barry! Jesus, what happened?'

'It was booby trapped. An incendiary device — small, but enough to give us a fucking shock,'

'Everyone alright?'

'Yeah, boss. We're just having a sit down for the minute.'

'Keep your team out of there. We'll get the bomb-disposal people down. I want to be sure there's nothing more.'

'Yeah, I agree. I don't think there will be, but better safe than sorry. The device lit up an armchair in front of the door with a dummy sat up in it. It must have been triggered when we opened the door. It was all about sending us a message.'

'Okay, Barry. Hold tight and let me make a few calls. I've arranged for patrols to get down there. Use them to evacuate the block and we'll get you and your men looked at by the ambulance people.'

'Patrols are just arriving by the sound of it. He's still fucking with us. This is his way of saying that he could finish us all if he wanted to.'

Darren sighed. 'No one's hurt though, Barry, that's what matters. Just hold tight, I want you all checked out.'

'I'm heading back. I'm fine. I'll leave the boys here, but I need to be back at the station.'

'Well, okay, Barry, but I don't need you if you want to stay with your team. Just keep me up to date, okay?'

'No problem.' Barry ended the call and got to his feet. He could see that his men were still in shock.

'Listen, boys, shit day. Sit tight for now, get checked over by the paramedics, they're on their way. The wooden-tops can sort out evacuating people and general bollocks and the bomb-disposal people can take over making the flat safe. Get yourselves together and head back when you're ready. I'm going back now, okay?'

Barry didn't wait for an answer.

He made it to the BMW, climbed in and rested his head on the steering wheel.

* * *

Tommy Wilkes was really getting into his role. He'd slashed his arm three times, and the blood was flowing nicely before anyone got to him. The moment the cell door opened, Tommy lunged at the officer with a razor blade in each hand. This earned him a couple of hits around the head and he backed away. It was a stand-off. He grinned bloodily at Jim the jailor.

The panic alarm suddenly stopped. An uncanny silence prevailed.

'Come on, Tommy, don't be stupid. Put them down and I'll help you out.' The jailer was breathing heavily. His cheeks were a blotchy red and his T-shirt was spotted with Tommy's blood. Tommy said nothing. He took a step forward and Jim immediately retreated. Another officer now filled the doorway.

'What's he got?' the officer asked.

'Razor blades,' said Jim. 'We're gonna need a Taser officer.'

The man turned and shouted down the corridor. 'Taser officer! Taser officer!'

Tommy grinned again.

* * *

George heard the shout. He knew that once a Taser arrived, it would all be over pretty quickly.

Kane was still in handcuffs. George took hold of his upper arm and they walked quickly towards the custody desk. The exit he needed was via a long corridor that jutted off to the right. George was afraid that someone might still be manning that desk. There were two exits, the other directly in front of them that led through into the police station. George could hear footfalls the other side of that door. As the first officer pushed open the door, he and Kane turned abruptly into the corridor and out of their line of sight. George silently prayed that no one was coming in from the yard. They made it to the door. In his panic, George swiped his pass too hastily and it didn't register. The second time he tried, the light turned green.

George hustled Kane towards a marked Skoda. He heard the door to custody open again, and someone shouted. They were shouting at him.

'George! What the fuck?' Matt Dobson stumbled as he came out of the door.

'Get in the car!' George screamed. Kane slid into the passenger seat. George reached behind him and took out Carl Matten's pistol. He'd almost forgotten he was still carrying it. He had tucked it in his waistband in case he got desperate for a plan B. With the weapon raised, George stepped towards Matt Dobson, who was running ran straight at him. Matt stopped dead.

'I don't have time to explain, Matt, but you know me, I wouldn't do this unless I had to.'

'Jesus, George, there's nothing to explain. We can still sort this out. Just bring him back in and put that fucking thing down.'

'You don't understand,' George said. He glanced back to the Soda. Kane was peering out of the window.

'Walk him back in, George. We can still sort this out.

'I can't.'

Matt had his hands spread out. He didn't seem angry or afraid of the weapon. More than anything else, Matt looked sad. George had betrayed him.

'Stay the fuck away or I will shoot you, Matt. Don't think for a second that I won't.' George hoped he sounded convincing.

'George, listen to yourself.' Matt took a step forward. George had no idea if the weapon worked, he hadn't thought to test it. He aimed a little high and to the right, praying that the sights weren't out. The gun went off all right, it kicked back hard. Matt dropped to one knee, his hands raised.

George ran back to the car. He could see the custody sergeant in the mirror, still kneeling and shaking his head. With a squeal of tyres, George Elms and Kane Forley powered away from Langthorne House.

Chapter 36

Matt sprinted back to the custody area. It was much calmer now. The disturbance had been neutralised and officers were smiling at the image of Tommy Wilkes stiffening and falling flat on his face as the Taser found its mark.

Jim the jailor noticed Matt's expression. 'Matt? What's up?' he asked.

Matt pushed past him into the office, snatched the custody radio from its cradle and pressed the emergency button. This would give him ten seconds of air time, with priority over all other calls.

'Control, we have a prisoner escaped from Langthorne custody. Kane Forley was taken out by DS George Elms. George Elms is in possession of a firearm. Repeat, for all patrols, George Elms is in possession of a short barrelled firearm. Shots fired as part of his escape, no injuries. Both males left in a marked Skoda patrol car, a sixty-four plate, I don't know the full reg. Is that received?'

'Yes, yes Langthorne custody, how long ago did this vehicle leave?'

'Zero two minutes,' Matt snapped back.

'Received that. Broadcast, broadcast, broadcast all patrols. For your attention, a prisoner has escaped lawful custody from Langthorne police station zero two minutes ago. DS George Elms is believed to be driving the prisoner in a marked Skoda patrol vehicle. George Elms is believed to be in possession of a firearm. All sightings to be reported to force control. No officers to engage without prior authority. Communication by mobile phone where possible please. Broadcast ends.'

Matt swore and threw the radio back onto the desk, where it hit a mug of coffee.

Over the radio came a cacophony of voices.

'This some sort of joke?' Jim managed. 'How the fuck does that happen?'

'We're closed, Jim. Get everyone out that doesn't need to be here. We don't take anyone else in.'

Jim nodded. 'You okay?' Jim said.

'Just get it done, Jim. I'll be fine.' Jim nodded again and left.

Matt slid down in the chair, with his hands over his eyes. 'Fuck!' he said again.

* * *

Barry Lance rolled to a stop at a junction. In his rear-view mirror he could see smoke still rising from Churchill House. The transmission from custody came through on his car radio. Barry let several cars go by while he thought. His stomach knotted. George had walked Kane out of custody in order to kill him. If he succeeded, Barry's wife would die. Barry stamped on the throttle and the big BMW lurched forward. In his haste, he had forgotten to activate his car's lights and sirens.

* * *

George turned the police radio off with a fierce jab.

Kane looked at him. 'What's the matter? You did it. You should be pleased.'

'Just tell me where we're going.' Sweat poured down George's forehead and ran into his eyes. He checked his mirrors yet again.

'You need to relax a little, George. This will all be over soon.' Kane wore a smile, and George turned to face it.

'I can't wait to wipe that smile off your fucking face, you know that?'

'I bet. That hate you have inside you right now, George, you be careful with that. It's taken me to some bad places.'

'I'm nothing like you.'

'Give it some thought when you have the time. You might reach a different conclusion.' Kane was still smiling.

George ignored the comment. 'Where are we going?'

'You know the old Eurotunnel building?'

'By the motorway?'

'Yes, head for that, but I would suggest staying off the motorway. The access is round the back.'

'Past the hotel. I know it. So is that where my family are?'

This seemed to amuse Kane. 'They're not in a hotel, George, but they are comfortable.'

'You think this is some sort of joke?'

'I am taking you to your family, George. Just like I promised.'

George fell silent. He peered out of his window, squarely into the wide eyes of Barry Lance, at the wheel of a black BMW SUV coming the other way.

'Shit!'

'What's the matter?' asked Kane.

George put his foot down. 'Unmarked police car. It saw us.'

'Lose them, George.'

George didn't reply. His mirror suddenly reflected the vivid blue of the BMW's lights. He watched Barry overtake two cars. He would soon be directly behind him. George activated the Skoda's blue lights. The chase was on.

George pulled away. He was able to take advantage of smaller gaps that the big, lumbering SUV wouldn't fit through. George knew he wouldn't be able to lose the BMW before he got to the old channel-tunnel site. Then he had an idea.

Two hundred metres ahead, a traffic light was on red. George pulled out into the middle of the road. The BMW was already forcing oncoming cars to brake, and those going the same way to veer left into the curb.

George made it to the traffic lights. He didn't stop at the red light. Instead, he cut across the traffic that was turning into his lane. All but one of the moving vehicles saw him. George struck a black Mini but ploughed on, ignoring the horns. The Mini came to a stop, right across the road. The BMW was stuck.

George powered on. The next set of traffic lights were green.

'I would suggest staying off the motorway,' Kane repeated.

'We can't go straight there if we want to lose 'em. We're too close.'

'You really think the motorway is the best place to do that? Surely, more of your lot will get to us faster?'

'Yeah, the traffic units will already be out on the coast bound side. I'm counting on it.'

Kane looked at him. 'You want more police?'

'You wanted us away clean. Now that means we need to lose the whole force. The only way to do that is to bring them all together.'

'See!' Kane grinned. 'Now you're starting to enjoy yourself.'

'Shut the fuck up and let me drive!' George turned the police radio back on. With the radio on, his car would appear on the mapping system and they would be able to track him. Which was just what he wanted.

* * *

'Control, this is Yankee One.' Barry Lance spoke through clenched teeth.

'Go ahead sir.'

'For all patrols, I am in command of this incident and all patrols are to act as eyes and ears only. No officers are to engage without my authority. Control, can you mark me up as ground command please? Last sighting Beachborough Road traffic lights, unsure of direction taken.'

'Understood — all patrols to be aware of the last. Inspector Lance is ground command and is mobile. All patrols are to report sightings of the suspect vehicle immediately and to take direct orders from Yankee One.'

Barry took his finger off the *talk* button. 'I'm going to get hold of this fucker and finish it, once and for all.'

2.

Chapter 37

Sergeant Ian Cannon was leading the chase for George and Kane Forley. He was an ex traffic officer, and clearly revelled in being centre stage in a live incident, even from his podium in a makeshift incident room.

Darren Lewis approached him. 'Where are we, Ian?'

'Right behind them, sir.' Ian put his hands behind him and straightened his back.

'He's on the motorway?'

'Yeah, heading right towards us. He won't be getting much further.'

'I assume we are looking to take him out on the motorway?'

'Oh yes, sir. Just as soon as I can get some guns in.'

* * *

George Elms' Skoda swept past the slip road leading onto the M20.

Kane looked out of the back window. 'Well, George, if you wanted every copper in the county up your arse, you've got your wish. I will remind you that we are also accelerating away from your wife and child at an alarming speed. You get me killed or arrested on this miserable stretch of road and your family's fate is sealed.'

'This is the only way, and anyway they're not *all* up my arse.' Sure enough the Skoda soon caught up with three identical police Volvos splayed out in a blocking formation, intending to slow him down.

'I assume this is where they make their move?' Kane was almost jumping up and down.

'I know the tactic.' George glanced in the mirror. The stream of police cars began to fan out across the road behind them. Two lead cars broke away. George was waiting for this to happen. These cars were the designated back and sides of a moving 'sandwich.' And George and Kane were about to become the filling.

George let them get close. Very close. He braked, and the cars were forced to veer apart. They started to drift past and George saw his opportunity. He braked again, skidded and brought the Skoda round to face the opposite direction.

The moving box was now at a full stop, all the cars facing away from their quarry. George drove straight towards the line of flashing cars that had been following them. Kane pushed his head back into the headrest and his right foot reached out for a non-existent brake pedal.

George headed straight for the car on the end of the row, next to the barrier. He didn't lift his foot. They side-swiped the car and then the barrier, the car bounced and scraped. But they were through. George picked up speed again, and the Skoda accelerated away into a clear road — going the wrong way down a four-lane motorway.

George was banking on the police sticking to the tactics he himself had been taught. They would have put a rolling road on further down and very soon he was going to come across a solitary police car holding up three lines of stationary traffic. They would be bumper to bumper, fifty cars deep by now. The Skoda screamed to 100mph. George daren't breathe. This had seemed like a good idea.

* * *

Darren Lewis listened to the radio report. George Elms had turned 180 degrees in the fast lane and was now powering back directly towards any number of civilian cars. Ian Cannon ran his hand through his hair. His earlier self-assurance had evaporated.

'Well, we can't pursue him,' he managed at last.

'So have you a plan B?' the chief demanded.

'Boss, we can't get behind him, it's a basic rule. When the target starts going the wrong way down a motorway, we call it off. It's suicide.'

'He knows that. That's why he's doing it.'

'I'm sure you're right, but I can't send anyone after him.'

Darren turned and called out into the room. 'What happened with the helicopter?'

'It's still fifteen minutes away, sir,' replied a woman officer. 'It was refuelling somewhere in Essex when the call went out.'

'Of course it was,' growled Darren. 'Ian, do we have *any* patrols the right side of George? The direction he's actually heading?'

'The firearms boys are all out of play, so are traffic. I'll try and get some local patrols to where they can at least watch him. Once we see where he comes off, we can start again.'

'Okay, fine. We'll track him and put out his position for the local patrols. Can we again reiterate that no one approaches that damned car. I want firearms to make it safe.' Darren's throat was suddenly dry.

One of the operators called out. 'Sir! We've lost him, sir. He was tracking southbound, but he's just disappeared off the system.'

'Of course he has. He's switched the radio off now he's led us up the garden path.' He turned to Ian Cannon. 'Ian? We're going to lose him, aren't we?'

Ian Cannon had no answer.

* * *

Barry Lance had had no choice but to hand over control of the pursuit to three firearms patrols who were given the task of bringing the Skoda to a hard stop. He just wanted to make sure he got to George Elms and Kane Forley as quickly as possible after it happened.

Barry had been held up at the traffic lights and then he found himself at the back of a clump of traffic brought to a stop to allow a sterile area for the pursuit to continue. He forced his way to the front of the jammed motorway just in time to see a damaged Skoda veer across three lanes of traffic and make for the hard shoulder. He'd heard the radio update and knew George had turned back. He'd also heard Darren Lewis call up to reaffirm that under no circumstances were any patrols to follow him. George and Kane were about to be lost to Lennockshire Police. Barry wouldn't get his wife back alive.

He couldn't let that happen.

Barry's BMW broke from the line of cars. A single marked Volvo sat in the middle of the road, slewed at an angle. The approaching Skoda slowed down and Barry saw his opportunity. The BMW surged across the front of the line of cars in a desperate attempt to block the gap. George accelerated hard. Barry could see Kane, wide-eyed in the passenger seat, staring at his BMW. The Skoda headed for the gap and Barry heard it strike the crash barrier. But it continued forward.

Barry Lance hit the crash barrier a split second later, head on. The BMW shuddered to a halt and Barry struggled out, shaking off the dust from his exploded airbag. He staggered a little.

The driver of the parked Volvo came towards him. 'Shit, sir. Are you okay?'

'I need your car.' Barry was tugging at the boot of the BMW while he spoke.

'Well, all right, but I should come with you.'

'Fuck that.'

The officer stood, mouth open. Barry pulled a G36 assault rifle out of the boot and slung it over his shoulder. He stuffed extra clips into his vest and patted his leg holster, which held a Glock pistol. He brushed past the officer, threw the rifle onto the Volvo's passenger seat and climbed in.

Barry was able to cut through a gap left by a couple of cars that had broken ranks in the confusion.

'This is Darren Lewis. Acting Chief Constable Darren Lewis directly to Barry Lance. Barry, please report in.'

Barry ignored the call. He shook his head, his senses still feeling a little dulled.

'This is Acting Chief Constable Darren Lewis. Inspector Lance — what are you doing?'

Barry switched off the radio. He wasn't sure *what* he was doing, but whatever it was, Darren Lewis didn't need to know.

Chapter 38

'Helen, this is my sister, Becky. Becky, this is Helen,' Mick said.

Becky stood in her doorway in a bathrobe and a pair of slippers that seemed too big for her. It was the middle of the afternoon. She looked Helen up and down, and frowned.

Helen shrugged. 'It's been a shit day.'

'Looks like it.' Becky stepped aside. 'My brother said you needed a bath, but that was an understatement. I'll find some leggings for you too, and I've a jumper that'll fit you.'

'Thanks, sis.' Mick kissed her on the cheek.

She stood with her arms folded. 'I guess I should know better than to ask what the fuck happened here?'

'Problems with the boyfriend,' Mick offered. 'Can I use your Wi-Fi?'

Becky's eyes narrowed. 'Are you the boyfriend?'

'No! Fuck, Beck, I'm not in the habit of beating up women, then bringing them round half-naked so my sister can clean them up!'

'Well, not normally. The Wi-Fi code's on the back of the box in the living room.' Becky shrugged and shuffled towards the kitchen. Mick beckoned and they went inside.

Becky's cottage was hidden away in a quiet part of the village of Westernhanger, on Langthorne's northern perimeter. It had a long drive and Mick was able to park the van out of sight.

'Nice place,' Helen called out. From the kitchen she could see a long garden with mature apple trees, this year's crop rotting on the ground. A wire fence enclosed an area of threadbare grass with chickens scratching at it.

'Thanks. The bathroom is just round the corner. It's a bit of an odd layout. Anyway, help yourself. I'll get my brother to knock us all up something to eat.'

Helen walked back to the bathroom. It contained a free-standing 'slipper' style bath beneath a large window with frosted glass. Helen pushed the door shut with her sore elbow. It caught Mick as he was coming in.

'What are you doing?' she asked.

Mick ignored her and went to the window. He locked it, pulled the key out and showed it to Helen on his way through the door.

'Just in case. There's a lock on this door.' Mick pointed to it. 'I will be outside. The second I hear it lock, I will kick it in. Do you understand?'

'Where would I be going, Mick? I suppose I could run and hide in the chicken coop in my underwear for a few days, then make a break for it when the weather improves! Don't be ridiculous.'

He didn't smile. 'Just don't lock the door, Helen.'

She held her hands up. Helen did smile, though, when she looked at the large bath. It was wonderful, with a tap that was designed so that the water cascaded out like a waterfall.

There was a light knock on the door. 'Helen — I brought you a drink.' Becky stepped in, holding out a large glass of white wine. 'I like a glass in the bath, and you looked like you could do with it.'

'Thank you, Becky, that's really kind of you,' said Helen, meaning it.

'And some toast.' Becky held up a plate piled with thick slices running with butter. 'My brother will do you something proper in a while, but this is just to keep you going. I didn't want you cutting your bath short because you're starving.'

'You're very kind.'

Helen was aware that Becky was lingering. She looked at Helen's body, with its ugly bruises and lacerations underneath the dirt and grime of the warehouse floor.

'Whatever happened to you, love, you make sure my brother sorts them out for it, yeah?'

Helen smiled. 'I will do, yeah.'

'I've got make-up an' that. Let me know when you need it, and you can have a dig about. But take your time in here, yeah?'

'Thanks again.'

'No problem.' Becky shuffled out of the room, those slippers dragging over the tiles.

Chapter 39

George needed to get back the way he had come. They were about two and a half miles from their destination and the queue of traffic was already longer than that. It was slow going, but he finally brought the Skoda to an untidy stop as far off the motorway as he could get. The front end of the car nudged a wooden gate that had once led to the rear of the channel-tunnel offices and a tract of Ministry of Defence land. It looked as though it was rarely used nowadays.

'We're about a mile out. We'll need to walk from here.'

'They'll spot the car and then they'll know where we are. I thought you had a plan for losing them?' Kane seemed amused, as if he were enjoying the situation.

'Means we don't have much time. I suggest we get going.' George untucked his shirt in an attempt to conceal the gun.

'These are going to cause me problems.' Kane raised his handcuffed arms. 'I reckon you could take them off for now, don't you? Especially as you appear to be armed.'

'You're still under arrest.'

'I may not be the only one before too long.'

'Get walking.' George pushed Kane towards the gate. He looked back at the queue of cars and saw a woman driving a people carrier staring at him. She looked away. George turned his attention to the wooden gate.

Kane struggled to climb it, forced to use his elbows to lever himself across. He fell to the ground on the other side.

George walked past him and grunted, 'Get up.'

They followed an overgrown track through an area of woodland. When they emerged, George could see a large building surrounded by a high perimeter fence. It looked vaguely sinister and out of place amid the cropland.

'This is the place, right?' George's heart raced, and he battled to hide his rising excitement.

Kane nodded. 'Yeah, there's a break in the fence on the east side.'

'After you.' Kane followed the track around the fence. George peered through and saw a large parking area that was gradually being reclaimed by nature.

'Here.' Kane lifted his handcuffed arms and gestured at the fence. George could see the place where it had been cut. Kane bent forward to step through, and George followed.

* * *

Barry Lance in the Volvo was reduced almost to walking pace. Impatient at the continuing delay, people had started to get out of their cars. They were everywhere, strolling into the road or stepping out onto the hard shoulder to try and see what the hold-up was. His marked police car attracted attention, and several people had tried to flag him down. A couple of times he had been brought to a complete stop by cars that had moved onto the hard shoulder. He was losing valuable time, and he could only hope that George was being held up in the same fashion.

‘Fuck’s sake!’ Barry swore as yet another member of the public stepped out to flag him down, a lone woman, standing beside a people carrier. He slowed but didn’t stop. The woman leant forward and put her hands flat on the bonnet.

‘Hey!’ she shouted.

Barry stopped and half-opened the window. ‘Out of the way!’ he bellowed.

She pointed off to Barry’s right. ‘Over there!’

He swore again and turned his head to see an abandoned Skoda, the passenger door wide open, standing in front of a farm gate.

‘They got out, went down there!’ the woman shouted again. Barry reversed and turned round, causing the woman to stagger. She swore at him but Barry wasn’t listening.

Barry parked against the rear of the Skoda, blocking it in. He made sure it was empty, then assessed the gate, and the chain that held it shut. He looked in the boot of the Volvo and found standard bolt cutters. They wouldn’t be enough.

‘Hey! What’s going on up there? Twenty minutes and we haven’t moved an inch!’ Barry heard footsteps coming towards him. He slammed the boot shut and moved round to the passenger door.

‘Hey! You listening to me or what? I got to get to work here!’

Barry turned towards the man, holding the G36 assault rifle pointed at his chest. ‘Fuck off!’ he growled.

The man lifted his hands and backed away.

Barry jumped the gate and broke into a jog. George and Kane had left a clear track of flattened grass for him to follow.

Chapter 40

The building loomed above them like a steel cliff face. They walked around it to a huge lean-to, covered with plastic. A loading bay. Kane stopped some twenty metres short of it. There were two lorry trailers parked under its cover.

'This is it,' he said. He turned towards George, his eyes flashing.

'This is what? Where's my family, Kane?'

'End game.' Kane smiled.

'No more games. I want my family.' George reached for the weapon. He was in control now.

'One more game.' Kane brought up his hands and raised his index finger. 'Two lorry trailers. Your wife in one, Barry Lance's in the other.'

'Barry? What are you talking about?'

'It's very simple. Your wife in one, Barry's wife in the other. No locks. You can just go up and take your wife away.'

'What about my daughter? Where's Charley?'

'Now, George, if she was here and you got to take her too, what would stop you shooting me dead with that nasty looking weapon in your hand?'

'George?' The voice was Sarah's.

'George!' she called again. George heard a scraping sound. He pushed past Kane and went to the back of the lorry on the left. Her fingers pushed through a small gap in the door. George reached out and held them.

He scanned the door quickly. It stuck out, there was a clear gap all the way around, the hinges on the side sticking out rather than lying flat. The door handles were thick metal bars pointing downwards.

'Don't open it, George. There's a bomb. If you open the door it goes off.'

'What?' His wife stood against the door. He could see some of her face, and she gave him a lopsided smile.

He turned to Kane, he raised the gun to point it at his chest. 'What did you do to her?'

'I needed to make sure she wasn't injured in the snatch, George. She's had a little chemically induced sleep but she won't have any ill effects. As long as you're not hasty.'

'What bomb?' George stepped down to face Kane. He pushed the barrel of the gun into Kane's forehead and fought the urge to pull the trigger.

'Who's there?' It was another voice, a woman George didn't recognise. It sounded weak.

Kane smiled. 'You should meet Barry's wife, George. She's a nice girl.'

George looked at the second lorry trailer, about twenty metres away. It looked identical to the one his wife occupied. The same pronounced door, but nothing visible through the gap at this distance.

'What did you do?'

'Nothing. Shelley's not a well woman. She's had a long fight with cancer. And from what I can see, it's not been going too well.'

'You stay still. Move off that spot and I will kill you.'

Kane shrugged. 'I have nowhere else to be.'

George glanced over to the trailer with his wife inside. He could see part of her through the gap around the door. She was standing, peering out.

He made it to Shelley. 'I'm George Elms. I'm a police officer, and I'm here to get you out of there. Are you okay?'

'Oh, thank God!' Shelley let out a sob.

'Are you okay?'

'I take medication. Pain medication. It gets pretty bad without it, I can't move much. I feel so damn useless.' George stepped closer and looked in. Shelley was sitting on the floor. Even in the poor light he could see that she was very gaunt. Her cheekbones protruded through her skin, and she was leaning on her elbows. Her breathing was laboured.

'Hold on,' George said. He paced back over to Kane.

'You should thank me really, George. You get to be the hero.' Kane's expression suddenly hardened. 'But only once.'

'What are you talking about?'

'The bomb. You've got a very real choice to make and time is not on your side. What is it now? It must be close to three, surely?'

George glanced at his watch. Sixteen minutes to three. 'What happens then?'

'Both charges detonate. No one can stop it. And we all need to be standing right back when that happens, George.'

'You said I would have a chance to save her! What chance?'

Kane tilted his head. 'You can go up to her now and walk her away. That's your chance.'

'You're fucking with me. I do that and the bomb goes off, right?'

'One of them does. It's simple. Open one door and the charge under the other detonates. I talked to the two girls about it before I left. I half expected to get here to find one of them had made the decision to walk away. You couldn't blame them for that, could you?' Kane smiled.

'You sick fuck.'

'My last chance to be anything, George. I'm *so* glad you're part of it.'

'Where's my daughter?'

'Solve your little conundrum here, George, and I will take you to your daughter.'

George felt the rage take him over. He grabbed Kane by the throat, and forced him backwards.

'You can kill me as many times as you want, but you won't get your daughter back,' Kane spluttered.

George hit Kane hard in the face. 'Where's Charley?'

'Fuck you, George. Make your choice and then we go get her.'

'No more of your games.'

'Tick-tock, George. A few minutes more and there'll be nothing left to choose from.'

George took a step back, raised the gun and pulled the trigger. The bullet tore through Kane's ankle. He screamed, and fell to the floor.

'Where's Charley?' George's voice was even and full of venom.

'Fuck you!'

George pulled the trigger again. This time the bullet penetrated the shin, shattering it and all but severing Kane's leg. He screamed again.

'Charley?' George said.

Kane rolled onto his side and clutched at his leg. George rested the barrel against the side of Kane's knee. Giving him no time to reply, he pulled the trigger. The joint exploded. Nothing remained of the knee but a red pulp. Kane rolled onto his front and whimpered. Afraid he might pass out, George put his foot on the bloody stump and pressed. Kane's eyes opened wide.

'My daughter. Or I keep shooting until I hit something you can't live without.'

Somehow Kane managed to laugh. 'You can be quite persuasive,' he said. 'It's too late anyway. She's already been handed over to a Romanian gang. They make good money from pretty little girls like that. They are expert at making children disappear. You'll never see her again.'

George stepped off Kane's bloodied leg and stooped over him.

'I know about Jana. I know she's our leak. She should have been picked up by now.' Kane raised his eyes and they met his. George had his confirmation. He stepped away from Kane so he wouldn't hear, and called Paul Baern.

'George! Jesus, I've been trying to call you for ages. What the hell's going on out there?'

'Paul, what happened with Jana? Did you get the message, did you—'

'Charley was there. That's why I've been trying to get hold of you. Charley was with Jana. I saw her come out and went over to talk to her, and she just fell apart. I took her back to her flat and Charley was sitting there with a glass of squash. But, George, what the fuck is going on?'

'Oh God.' George dropped to his knees. The phone fell from his hand and he bent forward, weeping. After a few moments he rocked back onto his heels. 'Sarah!' he called out. 'Sarah, Charley's fine! She's with Paul!' He picked up the phone again.

'Mate, look after her. Don't let her out of your sight.'

'Well, yeah of course. Is Sarah there? Where the fuck are you, man? The radio's going mental. It sounds like you're on the run again.'

'I owe you so much, Paul. Please, you have to trust me, just for a little while longer. I can't explain it all now, but it ends today.'

'You wanna speak to Charley? She's right here.'

George looked at his watch. Nine minutes to three.

'I can't talk to her now, mate, but I will real soon.

'I understand. Don't do anything fucking stupid out there, man. Just come home in one piece and explain it all to us, yeah?'

'Yeah, alright, mate. And, Paul?'

'Go ahead.'

'Stop swearing in front of my daughter.'

Paul was still chuckling when George cut the call. Kane was lying on his back, groaning. George aimed the gun at his forehead. 'Charley's at the police station waiting for us.'

'You're doing better than I thought,' Kane gasped. 'So now you get to kill me.'

'I don't have to. Tell me about the explosives.'

'What would you like to know?'

'How do I stop them going off?'

'One way or another, George, there is going to be an explosion.'

George settled on the left foot this time. The bullet hit the knuckle, and blew away three toes. Kane howled.

'Jesus, George!' Sarah shouted. He ignored her.

'Hold your hands flat against the ground.'

'Fuck you!'

'Do it.' George pushed the barrel of the weapon into Kane's mouth. 'I said hold your fucking hands out flat.'

Kane held out his right hand, palm up. He lay on his back and closed his eyes.

'I will keep shooting bits off you until you tell me something useful about that bomb, Kane. I know you. There is a way out. No more games.' He moved the gun and held it a few inches from the centre of Kane's hand. Kane's eyes flew open.

'It's only under her.'

George held the gun steady. 'What?'

'The charge. The only live one is under Shelley. Your wife's is just a barrel of water.'

George shook his head. 'Bullshit.'

'It's true. That stuff is volatile and I couldn't get enough for two. I didn't need to anyway.'

'So why under her? Why not Sarah? I'm the one you got the issue with.'

'You would have died with her,' answered Kane.

'That's my point.'

'I never wanted you dead, George Elms. What I want is for you to fucking suffer. I want you to be the one to fucking ruin another good man's life, kill his wife to save yours. I want you to *be who you are*.'

'Bullshit.'

'You can believe me or not, I don't care. Both doors trigger the charge in Shelley's trailer. Look at her, George, she's dead anyway. Go get your wife, and then spend the rest of your life pretending you did right.'

'And the timer? Three o'clock. Is that bullshit?'

Kane smiled, bloodily. The gun barrel had dislodged one of his teeth. 'Definitely not.'

George looked at his watch. Two fifty-six. He went back to his wife.

'What's going on, George?' Sarah said. Her voice was unsteady. He checked around the door, and then bent down to inspect the underneath of the lorry. Immediately he spotted two family size vanilla ice cream tubs screwed to the underside. Wires ran out of them up into the body of the trailer. A further two wires led towards the second trailer and another ice cream tub with a mobile phone strapped to the outside.

George called to them. 'I'm getting you out, just stay calm in there. Charley's fine, Sarah. Paul has her at the police station.'

'Is that safe? You said I wouldn't be safe at the police station.'

'It's okay now, honey. And she's with Paul.'

'Can't you call the bomb-disposal people?'

'Maybe, Sarah.' George glanced at his watch. Another minute had ticked by.

'Is there anything on the inside? Anything that's coming through from underneath the trailer, through the floor?'

Sarah called back. 'There's a metal barrel. Like a beer barrel, you know.'

'Okay.'

'He told me not to touch it. He said it was really dangerous.'

'Any markings on it?' George called out.

'Only what he wrote.'

'What's that?'

'T.A.T.P.,' Sarah said, 'and then a smiley face. You know what that means?'

'Possibly. Can you get close to it?'

'He said not to.'

'I need you to get close to it. I want to know if it has any smell.'

'What sort of smell?'

'Any fucking smell, Sarah! Just tell me!'

'Alright, alright, George. Give me a second.'

'Don't touch it. Don't open it or anything, just give it a sniff.'

George waited. He could hear his wife moving around. A few seconds passed. 'Jesus, George, I don't know. My nose is like numb, ever since he shoved something over my face and I went unconscious.'

'Shit! Okay, okay. Just stay away from it. Give me a sec while I speak to Shelley.'

Shelley had her mouth at the trailer door, as if she were trying to breathe in fresh air.

'How are you holding up?' asked George.

Shelley seemed to be struggling to focus. Her headscarf had fallen away and George could see her bald head, dotted with wisps of sandy coloured hair.

'I've been better,' she said, and gave him an exhausted smile.

'Shelley, do you know about this bomb?'

She nodded.

'I've tried to look, but I can't see inside. Sarah says she has a barrel in her trailer which would probably contain the charge. Have you got the same?' George leaned towards her.

Shelley spoke in a whisper, coughed and winced. 'He put it in. He wrote on it and told me it was explosive.' She coughed again. 'The bastard said it was made out of hair dye. Made a joke about too much dye making your hair fall out. As if I haven't heard them all before.'

She was holding onto the adapted hinge, and George placed his hand over hers. It felt icy cold. 'Everything's going to be okay, Shelley. We'll all be going home soon.'

'I'm not going home, George. You should just take your wife.'

'Don't be silly. I'm not leaving you.'

'What do I have to go home for? A lingering death. At least this way it will be quick, and it will have some meaning. I feel so damned worthless, George, nothing but a hindrance. Pull open that door and it's all over. Then I will have been worth something.'

'You've still got life in you, Shelley. And you are worth something. The barrel in there — does it smell of anything?'

'My sense of smell is really bad, it's a side effect of the treatment. But, yeah, it's a bit like bleach. Must be strong if I can smell it.'

'Thanks, Shelley. I'll be right back, okay?'

'Go get your wife, George. Be happy. There's nothing else.'

George squeezed her hand. 'I will be back.'

Kane was still lying on his back, writhing in pain.

'You may be telling the truth.'

'Imagine that.'

'You've got no more games to play now, Kane. You brought us both here so you could watch this play out. I won't give you that pleasure.' George levelled his weapon at Kane's forehead. His finger tightened on the trigger. Kane closed his eyes.

George heard a small sound. Something hit the truck over to his right. He turned, and saw a tiny bullet-shaped hole in the window. Another hole appeared in the door, along with a *thwack* sound.

'Don't you fucking move!'

George spun round towards the voice. Barry Lance was running towards him, wielding an assault rifle. 'The next one won't miss, George. Now drop your fucking weapon.'

George looked at the gun in his hand.

Kane managed to grin. 'Looks like you've got some explaining to do.'

'You don't understand, Barry,' George said.

Barry was three paces short of him. 'Drop it, or I drop you,' he said.

George did as he was told.

'Barry?' Shelley's voice was only just audible. Barry turned towards the trailer.

'She's here?' Barry looked down at Kane, who nodded.

Barry picked up George's weapon and ran to the trailer. His wife was peering out through the gap at the door.

Barry reached for her hand. 'Are you trapped in there? How does it open?'

'Impatient as ever.' Shelley gave him a weak smile.

'Oh, Shelley! I've been so worried about you, so worried. I thought I was losing you all over again.' He squeezed her hand tighter and then stepped back to examine the door.

'Is it locked?' Barry spun towards Kane and held up his gun. 'Is it locked, Forley?'

'It's not locked,' Kane called out. 'She's free to go.'

'Wait, Barry!' George shouted. He stepped forward, and Barry pointed the rifle at him.

'I told you not to fucking move!' he hissed.

George shouted back, 'There's explosives. If you open that door it goes off! The whole fucking place is rigged.'

'It's true, Barry,' Shelley called. 'He's fixed it so that if you open this door, a bomb under her trailer goes off.'

'What? There's not one under you?' Barry said.

'Yeah. If the other door opens.'

George took a step towards his wife. Barry fired into the ground between them. He brought the rifle higher.

'Walk away from the trailer. Go stand with your mate over there.'

George shook his head. 'I'm not moving. I'm not leaving her.'

Barry jerked the weapon. 'I think you should listen to the man with the rifle, George.'

'Jesus, Barry, she's my wife. If you're going to open that door over there, at least let me be with her when you do it.'

Barry seemed to be considering this. He fumbled at his vest and pulled out a pair of handcuffs. He threw them at George's feet.

'What do you want me to do with these?' George said.

'Put one on your wrist. Do it now, or I come over and do it for you.'

George picked them up and checked his watch as he did so. Two fifty-eight.

'Barry, don't you realise? We're doing exactly what he wanted us to do.' George gestured at Kane, who had now rolled onto his front to watch the show.

'And if I hadn't got here? Would you be working to get them both out, or would you have looked after yourself, like you always do?'

'They're both still here, aren't they? I was looking for a solution. There's very little time and we need to work together, not point guns at each other.'

'Three o'clock, George, that's what he told me. Did you know about that?'

'He knows!' Kane called out. 'He's trying to stall you, Barry, rush you into making a mistake. Devious fucker.'

Barry spun towards Kane and pulled the trigger. The bullet hit the ground.

'You don't believe this three o'clock deadline shit, do you?' George scoffed. He had snapped one handcuff onto his wrist and Barry came over and took hold of the empty one.

'Lift your hand up,' he barked at Sarah.

'No way.' She moved back into the trailer.

'It don't matter to me. I'll cuff him to the metal. I just thought you might want to be with him.'

'It's okay, honey!' George called out. Then he turned to Barry. 'What are you doing, Barry? Think! There must be another way.'

Barry shook his head. 'There isn't, is there? This has to end. Everyone that gets anywhere near you ends up dead or dying. You're like a curse. I need to walk my wife away from here, George. I know you understand that, at least. I'm sorry.'

'So am I. Maybe you're right. Maybe I am a curse. Just make sure everyone knows the truth about what happened here.'

Barry nodded. 'I can do that. But I can't lose her, George, we've been fighting so long.'

Sarah pushed her fingers through the gap at the door. George passed her the other cuff. He was now too far from the door handle to be able to reach it. Barry went up to George and patted him down for weapons. He took George's mobile phone and put it in his own pocket.

'It's time,' Barry said. George nodded. Barry patted his shoulder and stepped away.

Sarah's grip tightened. She whispered to him through the gap, her voice thick with fear. 'I don't want to die, George. Not like this. Not like this!'

George put his forehead to the gap. They were just touching.

'Trust me, Sarah. Everything's going to be alright.'

Barry moved back over to his wife. He put his hand on the trailer door handle.

Chapter 41

'X-ray Alpha one-one to control, are you receiving?'

The helicopter had come across the scene sooner than expected. They had cleared a canopy of trees after seeing two abandoned patrol cars just off the motorway. The on-board 'spotter', PC Sally Potts, noticed movement at the rear of a large building. At least three men, one of them in uniform, standing behind a lorry trailer and another lying on the ground, possibly injured.

'Go ahead X-Ray Alpha one-one.'

'Thank you, control, we have three persons at the rear of a building backing onto the motorway. It's a possible sighting but we came across it rather quickly. We are in the process of going back round, but we will climb out of range as a precaution.'

'Understood X-Ray Alpha one-one. Can you confirm your exact location, please?'

'Yes, yes.' Sally huffed a little. She was more interested in watching the scene below than bothering with map coordinates. The helicopter banked hard and Sally and the pilot looked down. They saw a sudden white flash and an explosion that engulfed everything around it in dirty smoke.

'Fucking hell!' Sally began transmitting to the control room. 'Explosion! There has been an explosion where activity was last seen. We no longer have visibility on the ground.'

Sally picked up her medic kit and had the door open almost before they landed. She bent double under the blades and ran out through the whirling dust and smoke.

Chapter 42

Dover's town centre was dead. Helen and Mick walked along the middle of the deserted high street between shuttered shops and 'To Let' signs.

Helen had heard Mick speak to his handler from his sister's house. They had been told to park in Stanhope Road in Dover. Helen had used a map to get them there. It was a steep hill with tightly packed terraced houses on either side. They were then instructed to walk the short distance to the town centre and down the high street towards the sea front. Mick was now awaiting further instructions.

Mick was nervous, Helen could tell. He kept checking over his shoulder. He eyed the smokers loitering outside the pubs. None of them seemed to take any notice. They got to Market Square, where the road opened up into a square with a defunct water fountain over a stagnant pool.

They crossed a road into a pedestrianised area that led away from the town centre towards the seafront. After a hundred metres or so the path sloped down into an underpass covered in graffiti.

'Smells of piss,' muttered Mick.

Helen shrugged. 'What underpass doesn't?'

They reached the bottom of the underpass and Mick's phone rang. He cast a furtive look around and raised it to his ear.

'Yeah?'

He walked just far enough away from her that she couldn't hear what he was saying. He spoke in a low voice. Helen leaned against the tiled wall. She was still limping, and her hands were cold. The hoodie she wore had been supplied by Becky, along with jeans that were a size too large. Becky had also unknowingly supplied Helen with a four-and-a-half-inch utility knife. Helen had deftly slid it out of the block in the kitchen when they'd sat down to eat their beans on toast. She kept it hidden in the front pocket of the hoodie.

Mick came back, looking even more jittery than before. 'We need to move.'

'Do we have a final destination yet?'

'No. We need to get back to the van.' Mick stood still.

Helen looked at him. 'Are you okay?'

'Yeah.'

'Something the matter?' Helen persisted.

'It's nothing. Maybe I'm just thinking too hard. I wouldn't put us back in that van. It's the one thing that can be linked to us.'

'And why have us walk down here and then make us walk all the way back again?'

'That part makes sense,' said Mick. 'Handlers often do that. I've sometimes been given the run around for days before a meeting. They walked us through an environment that was perfect for spotting anyone that might be following. They started us off in an area busy with traffic, and then into a pedestrian area that was much quieter. No one could have followed us in a car or on foot.'

'I didn't realise I was supposed to be looking out for someone tailing us.'

'You weren't. Neither was I. They would have their own spotters out. They must be satisfied that no one's interested in us.'

'Well, I'm very pleased for them. Walking isn't particularly comfortable for me at the moment, you know,' said Helen.

'Are you going to be okay? Walking back, I mean. We will have to take a slightly different route or it might look odd.'

She snorted. 'To who? Those drunks at the pub?'

'Who says they're drunks? Assume nothing.'

'Believe no one, check everything — the ABC of policing. I know, I know.'

Mick didn't smile. 'In the undercover world, that might just keep you alive.'

'And returning to the van?'

He shrugged. 'It's not ideal, but we don't have much choice. So can you walk okay, or not?'

'I'll be okay. Like you said, we don't have a choice.'

Mick tilted his head. 'True.'

* * *

Lisa Jones waited with her hands on the steering wheel while Emily Ryker finished her call. Emily sighed.

'He understands,' Emily said.

'Good.'

'I still don't understand why we're meeting there. Why not just get them into the hotel like I planned? Then we could have walked Mick out separate. It would just take a couple of officers, and Helen's in custody.'

'You've done really well here, Emily. I know this is your first time handling a UC asset. It's not an easy job. Our decisions come from a different perspective.'

'I think I'll stick to being a standard intelligence officer from now on.' Emily sighed again.

'You can do whatever you want after this, Emily. Pick your place, pick your job. We owe you that.'

'So what now? We get Helen in custody and then sneak Mick out of the system? He gets a new life somewhere and a desk job?'

Lisa shrugged. 'If there's one thing a UC asset is good at, it's plan B. He'll have the same option as you. We'll look after him.'

'And Helen? The press are going to be all over that when it comes out.'

'People forget. This is the end, Emily. Once we get Helen Webb, the force can start healing. She's the last open wound.'

Emily nodded. 'See you soon.' She opened the car door and stepped out into a strong sea breeze.

Lisa watched Emily walk away. 'Well, not quite the last.'

Chapter 43

'This is it?' Helen asked. They drove into a deserted car park at a beauty spot overlooking the English Channel. The busy port of Dover was clearly visible in the distance.

'Yeah.' Mick took the van as far into the car park as he could get. He backed up close to a mound of grass the same height as the van, effectively concealing it from the road.

Helen took in the view. 'Nice spot.'

Mick shook his head. His tension had returned in droves.

'Not where you would choose?'

'No. Not where anyone would choose.'

'Why? No one will see you with me, or when we meet the police. You're hidden.' Helen shrugged.

'Covert policing is all about hiding in plain sight. It's about having a believable cover story. We don't have that up here.'

'Best you don't get seen then.'

Mick's phone rang. Helen went back to looking out of the window. This time Mick didn't bother moving out of earshot.

'Yeah. Yeah, we're where you said. Yeah, she's still with me. I thought it was best to keep hold of her, you see.' Mick rolled his eyes.

'Okay,' he continued. 'Now? I'm not so sure this is the best place, you know . . . Hello? Hello?'

Mick lowered his phone. 'Well, she don't say much.'

Helen exhaled. 'This is it then,' she said.

'This is what?'

'Where I get arrested.'

'You're already under arrest.'

'You know what I mean. You don't normally get taken to a family member's house to have a bath and a new set of clothes.'

'True. There won't be much of that in prison. New clothes maybe.'

Helen smiled. It made her cheek hurt. 'Indeed. Thanks. For treating me okay. I know what you must think of me.'

Mick looked ahead. 'You have no idea.'

'They're not going to let you just walk away, you know. The Alcanis I mean. When they work out what you've done, they're going to come after you.'

'I know that.'

She looked at him. 'So why risk it all for me?'

'It wasn't for you.'

'To bring me to justice then? You're not one of those coppers that still believes in justice, are you?'

'No. At least, not normally. But if anyone needs to face the justice system, Helen, it's you. And besides all that, you provided me with an opportunity.'

'How so?' she asked.

'A few days ago the Alcanis killed an informant. He worked close to me, and was doing a similar sort of thing for them. They killed him and his wife, and I got wind that they were looking for his extended family so they could really send a message. Out of nowhere. I don't want to be looking over my shoulder, wondering if I'm next. At least this way I know they're coming for me. And I become Lennockshire Police's problem. With you in tow, they will have to protect me. They'll owe me that.'

'You really trust Lennockshire Police with your life?'

'I've got a better chance with them than without.'

'We'll see,' said Helen. She noticed Mick staring at her. 'What's wrong?'

Mick took hold of her wrist, unzipped his jacket and removed a pair of handcuffs. He snapped one on her wrist.

Helen snorted. 'You're joking! Fuck me, if I was going to run, I would have done it in that big open street, wouldn't I?'

'Maybe,' Mick said. 'But you've got a pretty bad limp and it would have drawn attention to us. I figure this is your last chance to give it a go. I don't want to have to deal with that, Helen. I think you've had enough rough treatment for one lifetime.'

'It's not necessary, Mick. I'm beat. Where would I go?'

Mick jerked his head. 'Free.' He took the other wrist and cuffed her hands together. He pulled off his jacket and laid it across her lap, covering the cuffs.

He gestured at her door. 'After you.'

Helen hesitated for a second, sighed and climbed out.

* * *

The building works on Dover's seafront were still in progress. Emily's car was parked behind a hotel at the opposite end of the promenade from Lisa's. She was glad of the walk, it would clear her head. The diggers and workmen had fallen silent. Soon the sun would disappear into the English Channel. She was in a reflective mood. Maybe she would sit for a while.

'Any job. Any place.' Emily shook her head. She wasn't used to so much choice. She wasn't sure if she liked it.

Her thoughts soon turned to Mick — or whatever his real name was. She had never met him, but his situation was so precarious that she worried about him. She definitely wanted nothing more to do with the world of covert policing. Not for a while at least. The knowledge that a simple mistake could have a massive impact on someone else's life was too much to take.

She saw a coffee shop on the other side of the road. A youngish man in black trousers and a white shirt was stacking chairs outside. Emily made her way towards him.

'Are you closed?'

The man gave her a warm smile. 'Not quite. You can have anything I can make in ten minutes.'

'How long does a latte take you?'

'Ten minutes.'

She grinned. 'I knew you were going to say that!'

The coffee was good. The man finished packing up the tables, leaving a single chair for Emily. The sun was in her eyes, so she shifted the chair into the shade.

Emily noticed a black Audi crawling alongside the kerb. The occupants were obviously looking for something — or someone. A silver Vauxhall, like the sort on a hire car fleet, approached from the opposite direction. The drivers of the two vehicles spoke through their open windows. Emily hid behind the stack of chairs. She could just about make out the words.

The driver of the Audi began to shout. 'She dropped her minutes ago! She's here somewhere! Find her!'

The Audi accelerated away. The silver Vauxhall carried on kerb crawling. Emily breathed in. They were looking for her.

'You okay?'

Emily jumped. She hadn't seen the waiter. He was still smiling, but it was slightly guarded.

'Yeah, I'm fine thanks.' She turned back to the road. The Vauxhall had come to a halt. Suddenly it began to reverse.

Emily stood up. 'Is there a back way out?'

The man nodded. The smile had disappeared completely.

'Thanks. Sorry about this.'

With a squeal of tyres, the Vauxhall drew to a halt, level with the café. Emily hurried inside, followed by the waiter.

He opened the rear door for her. 'Can I help?' He looked genuinely concerned.

Emily hesitated. 'Well, yes. If anyone comes and asks, you've just closed and no one was here. And when they've gone, call 999.'

'And say what?'

Emily took the waiter's order pad and pen out of his top pocket. She scribbled a few words and pushed it back. 'There's a name and a place.' She pointed at the name. 'Tell them this person is waiting at the place I've written. Tell them to send someone immediately.'

'Okay.'

'I can't tell you how important it is.'

The waiter nodded. 'Maybe one day you'll explain?'

'I will, yeah. It will take longer than ten minutes though.'

Emily heard footsteps approaching the café. Their eyes met, and the man picked up his broom. Emily pulled the door quietly shut behind her.

* * *

'Helen Webb! You're quite a legend, you know.'

'I'm sure you can think of a better label than that.' Helen stared unabashed at the speaker. The woman wore jeans, hiking boots and a fleece top. Her 'walking on the cliffs' outfit, thought Helen. The two strongly built men either side of her eyeballed Helen.

'I'm sure the press will do all of that for me,' said the woman. 'I'm DCI Lisa Jones. I have been called in to assist with the clean-up after the recent debacle down here.'

'I wouldn't fancy your job,' Helen said.

'I'm sure. The pressure can really get to some people.'

'Are you also going to be sorting out Mick?' Helen gestured at the empty space Mick had occupied before two other men led him away. Helen assumed it was for his own debrief.

'Not my remit, fortunately.'

'Let's get this over with then. The sooner I get through custody, the sooner I can start making myself comfortable in prison.'

Lisa didn't move. The two men stood firm.

'We can't put you in custody, ma'am.'

'What do you mean?'

'You're a bit of an embarrassment, see. So far we've been able to keep it pretty quiet. We've managed to deflect the media with the hunt for our cop killer. That will be resolved very soon, and it will be a big story. The papers and news channels will be full of it. Meanwhile, no one will even notice the discovery of a former senior officer, found at the foot of the cliffs at a well-known suicide spot.'

'Suicide . . . ?' Helen stammered. Her legs felt weak, and her heart began to pound.

'Suicide. We got a call from the Alcanis. Seems you sailed in there and offered them a deal, but it had no real leverage. So they called us and we were able to come up with a much more attractive offer. The Alcanis would deliver you, and we would have another look at the case against Alcani senior. Maybe we would notice a few holes in the case, enough for him to be released and sent back to Albania.'

'Deliver me? So here I am. You have to take me in!'

'We've learnt something from you, Helen. You've taught us that we don't *have* to do anything. We know all about what you offered as your bargaining chip, Helen. That information would have got officers killed, and you knew it. The Alcanis were supposed to deliver that too, but our Mick stepped in before they could get it from you. So now you have to do the right thing. You have to tell us where it is, and then you have to die.'

Helen looked around, wildly. 'This isn't happening. Tell me this isn't happening. I was desperate, I wasn't thinking straight.'

'Just think about what would happen if everyone got to know what you did. Your children would be able to read all about it when they got older. Meanwhile, you rot in a prison cell and spend the rest of your miserable life looking out. Is that what you really want? This is your best option, Helen.'

Helen shook her head. 'But there's so much that people don't know. I was just trying to protect the force!'

'Shit sticks though, Helen. Pretty soon no one's going to care what you did or why you did it. Where's the USB device you stole, Helen?'

Helen was silent. She looked out over the cliffs, her mind a whirl. It was a long way down.

'At least make some of it right, Helen. One of the people on that list was murdered in their own home just a few days ago, along with his wife. Because of you. Now. Tell us what you did with those files, Helen.'

The cliff face was uneven. A single rope marked the edge. Helen couldn't take her eyes off it.

Lisa stepped forward. 'This is your chance to repair some of the damage you did.'

'And if I tell you, you take me into custody. Is that the deal?'

Lisa shook her head. 'I think we're long past making any deals, Helen. No matter what you say you finish at the bottom of that cliff. But you will finally have done something honourable. You have my word that your memory will be treated with the greatest respect. Your daughters will grow up believing that you were something. Which is about the best someone in your situation could hope for.'

'That's not a deal. It's not anything.'

'We're running out of time, Helen. Make your choice.'

'This is murder.' Helen forced the words out. 'It will have to be, I'm not making it easy for you.'

Lisa shrugged. 'Then murder it will be.'

The two men stepped forward.

* * *

Mick had heard the sirens draw nearer. Two cars piled into the car park with their blue lights flashing. Flanked by his two male chaperones, Mick faced them. The first car seemed to be heading straight towards them. Suddenly Mick's two escorts broke away and ran in opposite directions.

Mick waited. The car door burst open.

'Are you Mick?' Another officer appeared above the car roof, looking around, apparently for the men who had fled.

'Well, yeah. What's the matter?'

'We got a call to say you were up here with Helen Webb. She's a wanted criminal, sir. Do you know where she is?' Mick was suddenly aware that the crew from the other car had circled around him. He was being penned in.

'You know Helen's here. I reported it. Your DCI is down there with her now.'

Two of the officers exchanged looks. 'What DCI?'

'Lisa Jones, I think she said. Is there a problem?'

'No. A misunderstanding, I'm sure.'

'Who's your informant?'

'Emily. That's the only name I have. Is there anyone here by that name?'

'Emily?' Why would his handler send an emergency response team? Mick didn't understand what was happening but he felt a sudden sense of urgency. 'They're down there.'

Mick ran. Three of the officers followed him. The ground was uneven, and he nearly lost his footing on the loose stones. It was a short sprint. Mick burst round a corner to see Helen Webb standing on the cliff edge. Two men stood with her. They had a lock on an arm each. She was pitched forward, her hands free of cuffs. She was sobbing, begging them to stop. A kitchen knife lay on the ground by her feet.

'What the fuck is going on?'

The two men turned and pulled Helen back from the edge.

'She tried to jump! Said she wanted to end it all.' Lisa Jones stepped forward. She sounded upset.

A uniform officer stepped past and took a firm hold of Helen.

'Helen Webb, you're under arrest for conspiracy to murder.'

Helen looked Lisa Jones in the eye. 'Shit sticks,' she said.

They led Helen away. She was smiling.

Chapter 44

'George, we have to stop meeting like this.' Sarah smiled at her husband and rested her hand on his forehead. George opened his eyes.

'You're in hospital, George. You're going to be okay.'

George's eyes moved round the room. His words were muffled by the oxygen mask covering his mouth and nose. Sarah pulled off the mask and laid it on the table beside his bed.

'Charley?'

'She's fine, George. She's here. I said she could come and see you when you woke up. I'll go and get her in a minute. Do you remember what happened?'

George struggled to sit up. 'There was a bomb. Kane, he—'

'Don't try and move, George.' Sarah stroked his forehead. 'Luckily, you were far enough away. The trailer exploded and you got a clout from the shockwave. You got a few bits of shrapnel too, the trailer broke up pretty bad. They pulled some pieces of plastic out of your side and your leg. Nothing that won't heal up okay.'

George moved his right hand and flinched. 'My hand?'

'Your wrist is broken. You were in handcuffs when you got knocked off your feet. Your wrist must have taken all your weight. It will heal, George. It will all heal.'

'What about you?'

'I'm okay. A bit traumatised. The side of the trailer was all bent in — you should see it — but nothing got through. It shook me off my feet and I banged my head, but it's nothing.'

'What happened to Kane? I hurt him bad.'

'Dead. They don't know when, whether it was before or after the explosion, but I get the impression they don't care too much.'

George sighed. He ran a hand through his hair. 'I'm in a lot of trouble.'

'I don't think so. I spoke to someone in charge. They said it's pretty clear what happened. You'll just need to give them some more details.'

'I shot at a sergeant on police premises. They'll definitely have the hump about that.'

'Did you hit him?'

'No. I was only sending a message.'

'Whatever you did, it was because you had to. I was certainly very happy to see you when you turned up.'

George was silent for a while trying to piece together what had happened.

'Barry? And his wife?'

'Both gone. They would have taken the full force.

'Jesus.' George grimaced.

'You knew, didn't you, George?'

George had his eyes tightly closed. 'Knew what?'

'The explosion. You knew it would be that poor woman's trailer. That they would both die if he opened that door.'

'I couldn't know.'

'You did. I still remember the way you looked at me when you told me everything was going to be fine. You knew Kane had lied to me about the bomb.'

'I couldn't be certain.'

'But you had a pretty good idea.'

George opened his eyes. 'He told me. When he was on the floor and I had my foot on his leg. I'm good at reading people, and I didn't think he was lying.'

Sarah looked into his eyes. 'You let them die.'

'I tried to talk to him.'

'Why didn't you tell them? There might have been something we — you — could have done.'

'Like what?'

'Anything. Anything but letting them blow themselves to smithereens. You let them die.' Sarah raised her voice.

'I let us live.'

'Why couldn't we all have lived?'

'The device was on a timer. I couldn't stop it going off. Kane meant for her to die. He wanted me to live with that for the rest of my life.'

'But her husband! He could have been a hundred metres away when it went off.'

'He wouldn't have been though, Sarah. He would have been standing right with her, just like I was with you.'

'Why not tell him?'

'Because he was terrified. He had a high-powered rifle, and it was a hopeless situation. As he saw it, I was the whole reason he was there in the first place. And . . . and because I thought that if I just held your hand as tight as I could, it would all be over, either way. And I was right.'

'I don't recognise you sometimes, George, I really don't.'

'I don't recognise me either, Sarah. I will do anything for you and for our daughter, for us to be a family again. I want what we had. I don't mean for people to get hurt, Sarah, that's the last thing I want.'

George reached out and they clasped their hands together.

'A lot of people have got hurt around me,. I never intended for any of it. I was just trying to protect you. And Charley.'

Sarah managed an exhausted smile. 'I'll go get her. She's been dying to see you.'

THE END

Thank you for reading this book. If you enjoyed it please leave feedback on Amazon, and if there is anything we missed or you have a question about then please get in touch. The author and publishing team appreciate your feedback and time reading this book.

Our email is office@joffebooks.com

www.joffebooks.com

LANGTHORNE SERIES
BODILY HARM
PANIC BUTTON
BLOOD MONEY
END GAME

18897962R00137

Printed in Poland
by Amazon Fulfillment
Poland Sp. z o.o., Wrocław